BROWNING TAKES OFF

Peter Corris was born in Stawell, Victoria, in 1942. From 1964 to 1975 he taught history at Monash, ANU and the University of Melbourne. He has been a professional writer since 1975 and was literary editor of the *National Times* from 1978 to 1980. He lives in Sydney's inner west, works in a city flat and relaxes in the Blue Mountains.

By the same author

The Winning Side

'Cliff Hardy' series
The Dying Trade
White Meat
The Marvellous Boy
The Empty Beach
Heroin Annie
Make Me Rich
The Big Drop
Deal Me Out
The Greenwich Apartments
The January Zone
Man in the Shadows

'Richard Browning' series
'Beverly Hills' Browning
'Box Office' Browning

'Pokerface' series
Pokerface
The Baltic Business
The Kimberley Killing

BROWNING TAKES OFF

From tapes among the papers
of Richard Browning

transcribed and edited by
Peter Corris

ISBN-13: 9780140121599
ISBN-10: 0140121595

FOR
Patrick Cook

INTRODUCTION

The transcribing, copying and editing of the Browning tapes proceeds smoothly. The work has been facilitated by a generous grant from Mr Richard Kelly Featherstone of New York City who wrote to me after the publication of the second volume of the Browning memoirs. Mr Featherstone was born in Providence, Rhode Island in 1923 and was raised by a couple whom he believed to be his parents until their deaths in a motor car accident in 1965. By this time Mr Featherstone, who had been educated at an exclusive military school and Harvard University, was a prosperous attorney. His first letter to me reads in part:

As I was sorting through my parents' effects I came upon evidence that I was not their child but some sort of changeling whose support had been handsomely subsidised by a person whose name was not recorded. I have to say that their performance of the role of parents was beyond reproach. I had love and respect from them and I gave it in return and still do. Nor was there any sign that they had profited personally from the task of bringing me up.

My father, Mr Henry G. Featherstone . . . was an attorney and a successful one. I was proud to follow the same profession. The point, Mr Corris, is that I was a round peg in a round hole (although my children might think to substitute 'square' for round) and I had no reason ever to suspect that I was not a Featherstone born and bred.

I have been unable to find out anything about the source of the funds that helped to educate and cultivate me, beyond two things. One, they ceased when I reached the age of twenty-six. I was a qualified lawyer by this time of course and no longer dependent on my parents, although this was only recently true as I had pursued postgraduate studies and had undertaken some improving travel abroad. Secondly, one paper among my father's effects carried the name 'Bonnie Dalton', written almost as a doodle or jotting.

Mr Featherstone read *'Beverly Hills' Browning* and became convinced that he was the offspring of Richard Browning and the woman referred to there as Bonnie Dalton. As readers of that book will know, my efforts to trace Bonnie Dalton, a bit part actress in the Hollywood of the 1920s, failed and Mr Featherstone's history may provide a clue to her later life. It seems possible that she was a kinswoman of the Featherstones and came to an arrangement with them about the child. She must have remained prosperous for twenty-six years to have contributed so handsomely to her son's upbringing. (According to Mr Featherstone, his benefactor met all school and college fees and a great many other expenses.) She also may have stayed in touch with the Featherstones and received reports on the boy's progress. Alternatively, the cessation of the allowance may have been occasioned by her own death rather than any awareness of Mr Featherstone's independence.

Mr Featherstone is continuing research into the circumstances and documentation of his birth (he regards his given names as further proof) and following other scanty clues. Meantime, I have to express my deep gratitude to him for the support he has lent to the project. He has given generously and asked for nothing – certainly he wishes 'Box Office' Browning's memoirs to be published in full and without censorship of any kind.

The usual problems have been encountered in preparing this portion of the record of Richard Browning's life. Unfortunately, he seems to have used some inferior cassettes and poor voice quality has sometimes resulted. As a consequence it is sometimes difficult to discern words and phrases, particularly when Indian and Eskimo names are involved. It seems likely that Browning, decades after these events in the 'frozen north' and working without the benefit of notes, was often simply guessing and many of the names he gives have been unlocatable in the ethnological literature. There are other quirks too: in tapes covering the early period Browning appears to shudder as if with the cold and leaves off taping apparently to get up and close a door or window. At later points, especially when affected by liquor, he imitates the sounds of aircraft, often to the detriment of clear recording and transcription.

For help with aspects of aviation history in the period covered by Browning's memoir I am grateful to Trevor Thom, an enthusiast.

P.C.
Sydney, 1989

CONTENTS

CHAPTER ONE

If your idea of a Mountie[1] is a guy in a scarlet coat on horseback tracking renegade Indians and Eskimos, rescuing girls from avalanches and crooning 'Rosemarie' to them, you're way off beam. For one thing, a lot of the work of the Royal Canadian Mounted Police was done by motorised transport – cars, boats and even planes. There was a good deal of walking in snow as I was to find out to my discomfort, and in one particular respect the real Mounties differed completely from the movie version – I never met one who could sing.

I'd fetched up in British Columbia in a stolen ketch named the *Darwin*. Stealing the boat was no big problem as I'd stolen it from some bootleggers who'd coerced me into helping them land booze in California. And Canada was the right place to be – a thousand miles from LA where a misunderstanding over a woman (what else?) had caused the local leader of the International Workers of the World to hate me worse than capitalism. The real problem was that my servant Pedro Cortez and I had dropped off a Latin bootlegger on the American side of the border. So what? Well, he happened to have a Thompson submachine gun with him and my middle name happened to be Kelly. The Mounties were on the look out for gun runners, illegal immigrants and drug smugglers so Inspector Ambrose Chester had nabbed me for a gun-running, seditious Fenian. I guess they hoped they'd find some drugs aboard the *Darwin* to complete the package.

Nabbed is the right word because, after I'd taken in the situation and stumbled up onto the dock from the *Darwin,* I followed my natural instinct in tight spots, which is to run. A well polished and smartly stuck-out boot put an end to that. I sprawled on the wet, greasy planks and looked up at the knife-edge crease in Chester's pants.

'Sorry,' I said, 'must've slipped.'

Chester and his underling bundled us into a car and we drove through the city to the police lockup. I didn't see much of Vancouver on that trip – the day was fine but the air was cold and seemed foggy. I learned later that the place is famous for its fogs. There was a sort of arraignment room in a basement under the police building and Chester took us there practically on the run and raced through some mumbo-jumbo in front of a scribbling clerk and another official who nodded and tapped his desk with a pencil.

Tap, tap, he went. 'To be held for committal.'

'Wait on,' I said. 'This doesn't sound like British law to me.'

'Know a bit about it, do you?' Chester said. 'I'll just bet you do. Well, this is *Mountie* law for now, mister. You'll see some of the other kind soon enough.' He barked an order and Pedro and I found ourselves marching between two stalwart Mounties out of the room and down some steps to the cells.

It was cold down there and pretty dark. There were three or four cells, all empty, and we were put together in the biggest one which had four bunks and two buckets. One of the Mounties looked at me oddly as they closed the door and I thought to take advantage of it. 'What about a smoke?' I said.

He looked at me again, shrugged and felt in his pockets. He tossed a packet through the barred upper half of the steel door to the cell and placed a couple of matches on top of the heavy lock.

'Thanks,' I said.

Pedro hadn't said a word the whole time, limiting himself to nods and shakes of the head when asked things like, 'Are you a

British subject?' Now he pulled a blanket off a bunk, wrapped it around himself and glowered.

'A cigarette, por favor,' he said.

I lit the cigarettes and Pedro blew a stream of smoke at some bugs clustered on the cell wall.

'We're in a bad fix,' I said.

He nodded. 'Different fixes but bad for both. I don't think they will charge me with the gun running.'

'Oh, why d'you say that?'

He smiled; his teeth were white against his dark, bearded face and he brushed his hair forward. 'No speak English,' he said.

I had to laugh. 'You're a cunning bastard, Pedro.'

'Not so cunning perhaps. I suppose they could send me back to Mexico?'

'Probably.'

'That means I'll be shot. What do they do to gun runners and seditionists here?'

'Shoot them, I imagine.'

I used the bucket and sat on a bunk smoking and wondering if the place provided meals. I was starving and also feeling badly in need of a strong drink. I could stave off the hunger and the craving with cigarettes but then I'd run out of them and be left with another craving. I mulled this over and sneaked another cigarette while Pedro had a nap. We must both have looked pretty villainous – shaggy haired, bearded and dirty. I was wearing only two thin shirts and a light jacket, so I followed Pedro's example by wrapping a blanket around me. It was a miserable hour, sitting hunched in the cold cell like an Indian waiting to be sent back to the reservation, or worse.

I was thinking about another smoke when the Mountie who'd given me the cigarettes appeared at the bars with a steaming enamel mug. I jumped up and he lifted his finger to his lips to indicate silence. He passed the mug through the bars and I sipped strong, hot, sweet coffee for the first time in weeks. He peered in at me and stroked his smooth, clean-shaven face.

'My name's Connybear,' he said.

'You're a gentleman, Constable. I'm pleased to meet you.' I was willing enough to suck up to him for a few more cigarettes and another mug of coffee even though I knew what was coming – some God-bothering sermon unless I missed my guess.

'I was up in the Yukon[2] one time, prospecting.' He was a softly spoken man and I had to lean closer to listen, not that I was very interested.

'Yes?' I drank more coffee.

'Yeah. Grew a wild beard and hair like yours; just like yours. Dang me if we wouldn't look like twins if'n I was like that now.'

I looked more closely at him. He was a few years younger than me and it had been a long time since I was clean-shaven but I could see a strong resemblance in eyes, shape of face, hair and so on. 'Yes,' I said. 'You're a handsome devil, we're much alike.'

I thought I heard a grunt from Pedro but it might have been a snore.

'Thing is,' Connybear said, 'have you got any scars under all that hair? Got any pock marks or anything?'

'Certainly not!'

He gripped the bars and practically thrust his face into mine. 'I want to get outa the Mounties,' he whispered. 'I hate it.'

'Well, can't you resign?'

'I'm signed on for another six months an' I don't think I can take it that long.'

'I'm sorry. Any more coffee?'

He poured from a metal pot and offered his cigarettes. I took a deep drag and a long swallow of the coffee. 'You wouldn't have a drop of something, would you, Constable?'

He nodded, took a silver flask from his jacket pocket and poured a solid slug into my mug. I drank again and felt the warmth of the brandy running down my throat and into my stomach and through the length of me. Wonderful. Maybe he had a woman tucked away behind the nearest door. I felt relaxed and vaguely interested in his plight. 'What's the matter with the job? Too hard?'

'No, too boring. Just a bit of this and a bit of that. No real work. It's no work for a man at all.'

'That's too bad. Well, six months isn't long.'

'It's too long for me! How would you like to get out of here tonight?'

Careful, Dick, I thought, *he has a fanatical look to him.* 'Well, I suppose . . .'

'Tonight!' he said fiercely. 'You and your friend.'

'How?'

'By turnin' yourself into me. See, I let you, that is, me, escape. You take a knock on the head or somethin', an'. . .'

'Hold on. You mean I impersonate you?'

'That's right. See, I haven't been posted here all that long. No one knows me that well. I could fill you in real quick on what goes on around here. You could do it. Ever done any actin'?'

'Si, señor,' Pedro said from the darkness. 'He is a movie star.'

Connybear jumped at the sound but recovered quickly and grinned. It was uncanny; the slow smile spreading across his face was like the one I'd seen in photographs of myself a hundred times. Pedro came forward and accepted a cigarette. He took the mug from my hand and held it out for Connybear to wield the flask.

'It'd be a piece of pie to you, then,' the Mountie said. 'You can ride, can't you? Shoot a bit?'

'I thought you said it was all dull work, mooching around this place?'

'Sure. Mostly.'

I was tempted but deeply suspicious. Would someone trade places with a man likely to be convicted of capital offences all because of six months unpalatable duty? Not likely. Some other motive then. What? Money.

'You mentioned the Yukon, Connybear. Are you sure you don't want to rush up there for some reason? Are you sure you don't *need* to get out of the police for some reason?'

His eyes went cunning and narrow. If I was going to impersonate him I'd have to work on that – a wide-eyed, disingenuous look is more my style.

Connybear scratched his smooth chin. 'Well . . .'

'What does it matter?' Pedro said. 'It sounds like a wonderful plan.'

'Shut up. Well, Constable Connybear?'

'You got me,' he said. 'I could throw in a hundred dollars. It's true I've got a reason. It's not gold, mind you, more chancy. But still, I have to get out of the service.'

'You're not facing some trouble yourself?' I took the mug from Pedro and finished the laced coffee.

'No, no. D'you think they'd trust me to be turnkey like this if I wasn't in good standing?'

'Take his offer,' Pedro hissed. 'You owe it to me!'

'What's the plan?' I said.

Connybear suddenly became very excited. 'I bring in hair cutting tackle an' shavin' gear and we get you all cleaned up. Then we change clothes, we're so close in size as to make no difference. I saw that in the court. I let you out an' wallop you on the head. Not too hard. But we make it look like you got careless an' I hit you an' got the keys. Then your friend . . .'

'Pedro Cortez,' Pedro said.

'Pedro and me skedaddle. We get the boat an' take off.'

'Leaving me to face the music.'

Connybear emptied the flask into the mug and gave it to me. 'You'll have nothin' to worry about. You can be dazed an' confused for a few hours while you get your bearin's and see what's goin' on.'

'What if someone shows up in the middle of all this?'

'No chance of that. They're all over in the barracks where it's warm. Only prisoners and poor ol' guards have to hang around in this cold crib.'

'Foolproof,' Pedro said.

'It's all right for you,' I said. 'You're taking off in the boat, no doubt with more brandy and a head start.'

'Few hours,' Connybear said. 'What choice've you got? You're facin' twenty years in Manitoba prison, that's if you're lucky.'

'Make sure you bring the money,' I said.

Connybear came back an hour later and he and Pedro cut my hair and shaved me. Connybear took the clippings and said he'd get rid of them. The resemblance was amazing. I was a little paler where the beard had been but otherwise we were like twins. I fancied my teeth were a fraction straighter and whiter. Connybear's uniform fitted perfectly. He shrugged into my clothes and scratched himself.

'When'd you last wash these duds?' he said.

'I forget. Where's the money?'

'In your pocket.'

I took out the roll of notes and counted them. The cell door was open and Pedro was standing there with an unlit cigarette in his mouth. 'Well, good luck, Dick,' he said. 'I'm sure we'll meet up again.'

'Hope so, Pedro.' We shook hands and then something landed on the back of my head. It felt like the steel door of the cell; the strange-feeling boots slipped from under me and the steel door hit me again.

CHAPTER TWO

When I came around it seemed as if I was lying in the middle of a dense, cold patch of Vancouver fog. Faces came swimming towards me through the vapours – my wife, Elizabeth, Pedro, Inspector Chester, Connybear – it was hard to tell what was real and what was not. Eventually two faces assumed solid and believable form – Chester's and that of another Mountie.

'Connybear, are you all right, man?' Chester rapped.

'Er . . . oh, I think . . .'

'He sounds funny,' the other one said.

I had wit enough to realise that he was talking about my accent which, I suppose, was Australian overlaid with some Californian by now. I opened my eyes, blinked and let my head roll to one side. *Better do some listening before I do any more talking,* I thought.

'Plain enough what happened here, Connors,' Chester said. 'This damn fool got drunk and got careless. That Browning is a desperate fellow and no mistake. And it's a wonder the Mexican didn't knife him into the bargain.'

'It looks that way, sir,' Connors said.

Apart from the drunkenness accusation, grossly unjust that, this analysis didn't sound too bad. If I kept my wits about me perhaps I could pull this mad stunt off. I groaned and twitched, drawing my legs up and letting them flop down again.

'D'you think he's got a brain injury, sir?'

'Never had any brains that I ever heard of,' Chester said. 'What's the time?'

'Six o'clock, sir.'

'Damn them! They must have five or six hours start at least. Well, telephone the dock and secure that boat of theirs. Send someone to the railway and put a few men on the trucking yards.'

'Yes, sir. What about Connybear?'

'Get a stretcher and take him to the infirmary. Oh, and pick up that flask and bring it to my office. That's solid evidence against him.'

I kept my eyes firmly shut but I ground my teeth with anger. That bastard Connybear had nobbled me.

'He's grinding his teeth, sir.'

'He'll be grinding rocks if I have anything to do with it, and for the whole of his service. How long has he got to run, by the way?'

'He re-enlisted last week, sir,' Connors said. 'Three years, unless he buys himself out.'

'Permission refused,' Chester grunted.

I think I fainted or I might just have blacked out from frustrated rage. I was too trusting, that was my trouble. And Pedro had pressured me. I had some money on the boat; I could have hired a lawyer. Then I thought about the boat and Connybear and Pedro. Goodbye boat, goodbye money.

The next thing I was conscious of was a hard but warm bed and a smell of disinfectant. The smell was like that in the army medical tents I'd had to visit for odd scratches and when I'd been malingering during my service in the Great War. The smell usually made me feel sick which had helped me to malinger convincingly but it brought back too many bad memories now. I wouldn't be able to malinger for three years and I wondered how harsh Mountie discipline really was. My head throbbed and I felt a burning in my throat. I opened my eyes; I was in a small room containing one other bed which was empty. The single window was set high up. The floor and walls were bare and the furniture was a plain cabinet beside each bed.

'Water,' I croaked. No response. I tried to shout, 'Water!' and the effort caused a shattering pain. I whimpered the word again. An orderly dressed in a white coat and wearing a knitted woollen cap pushed open the door and approached the bed. 'What did you say?'

I tried to get a little of Connybear's soft, vaguely Irish accent into the words. 'Water. Water, please.'

'Why, sure. Here you are.' He took a carafe and a glass from the cabinet and poured. Then he raised my head and helped me to sip from the glass. 'How bad's the head?'

'Real bad.'

'I could give you a pill. A little morphine maybe?'

I nodded. The movement let fly ricocheting bullets of pain inside my head and I groaned. I felt something cold on my tongue.

'Yup,' the orderly said, 'this is what you need. Just swallow it down with a little water and lay back easy.'

I did it. There was a booming in my ears that suddenly stopped; my head felt light and a sweet warm feeling stole up from the soles of my feet. I saw soft glowing lights and heard sweet music that kept getting sweeter and sweeter but further away . . .

When consciousness returned things were a lot worse. There was a dull ache in my head, I had a raging sore throat and three men dressed in the full magnificence of the uniforms of the Royal Canadian Mounted Police were standing around my bed. Two of them had more insignia on their jackets than Chester – the real top brass.

'Connybear,' Chester said, 'this is Superintendent Anderson and Assistant Commissioner Cartwright.'

'Sirs,' I said weakly.

'I hope that is not intended as a joke,' Cartwright said. He was a dark-haired block of a man with shoulders like a bull moose.

'No, sir,' I said, trying to copy Connybear's accent.

'This is a serious matter, Connybear,' Anderson growled. He was smaller than the other two and fairish with a sharp, inquisitive face. 'A dereliction of duty charge carries a serious penalty. And we have complications. That villain Browning . . .'

'Yes, yes,' Cartwright cut in. 'But our object is to try to contain the damage, is it not? Chester?'

'Quite so, sir,' says Chester, toadying away like mad. They all do it in my experience, right up to Field Marshall.

'Drunk on duty and allowing prisoners to escape,' Anderson said. 'It's a stockade offence.'

I couldn't let them get away with that. I shakily extracted one hand from beneath the bedclothes and raised it to my head. As it happened I'd skinned the hand in my fall and it was bandaged – so much the better. I kept my voice just above a cracked whisper. 'I have to say, Mr Commissioner, that allowed isn't quite the word. I was savagely attacked. An' I only took a sip . . .'

'All in mitigation,' says Cartwright, who was beginning to seem more reasonable by the minute. 'I do not have to tell you, surely, that these are difficult times for the Force. Strange, un-Canadian, lax ideas are abroad. As I say, we have to think of the reputation of the Force and *contain* this thing!'

'What thing?' I hadn't quite got into the way of it yet. 'Sir,' I added.

Chester frowned thunderously. 'Browning, whom you allowed to escape, along with his nigger partner, held up and robbed three people on the way to the boat dock. There they assaulted and robbed the nightwatchman. They stole fuel and they started a fire which damaged the wharves extensively.'

'I hadn't heard about the assault and the fire,' Cartwright said. 'Well, thank God for that!'

'What do you mean, sir?' asks Anderson.

'These men are obviously desperate and experienced terrorists. It was hardly to be expected that one man could guard them effectively.

They could no doubt pick locks and possibly had concealed weapons. The responsibility for this must be shared, gentlemen.'

'Shared?' gasped Chester. 'Connybear got drunk, he . . .'

'They could well have drugged the drink.' Cartwright moved his shoulders as if he was about to batter down a door. 'Inspector Chester, as arresting officer you should have examined the prisoners more carefully, and mounted a heavier guard.'

Chester snapped to attention. 'Sir!' he said.

I tried to remain impassive but it was hard to do so under Anderson's malevolent stare. 'D'you mean, sir,' he said slowly, 'that this negligent wretch is exonerated?'

'Oh, no, Superintendent. Far from it. Constable Connybear will spend a considerable time in hospital recovering from the wounds he incurred in his gallant struggle with the terrorists.'

I couldn't help it; a small smile escaped me at the looks on Chester's and Anderson's faces. But the Assistant Commissioner hadn't finished. 'And when Constable Connybear *has* recovered,' he went on, 'he will be posted as far north as the writ of the Royal Canadian Mounted runs and his superior officer will be instructed to keep him on patrol for twelve months of the year!'

He spun on his heel and marched out. Anderson followed him and Chester remained, still at attention. When the others were out of the room he relaxed. A terrible smile spread over his waxy features and for a minute I thought he was on to me but he twitched his moustache and brought his face down close to mine. I could smell tobacco and brandy on his breath. 'You will wish you had never been born, Connybear. After one year up there, let alone three, you will begin to grow fur!'

He followed his superiors out of the room. The bed suddenly felt hard and I shivered despite the thick blankets. My head ached unendurably and even the scraped hand smarted. My mouth was dry and my tongue felt like a pound of raw steak. 'Orderly,' I croaked, 'morphine! More morphine for the love of God!'

CHAPTER THREE

First there was the boredom. I was fully recovered after a couple of days and I was keen to move around the place, get to know it and, more to the point, get to know the way out of it. But this was not to be. Connybear and Pedro had got clean away in the *Darwin,* leaving robbed and assaulted men and a burning dockside behind them. I was the gallant survivor of the whole episode and had to play my part. They bandaged my head and I only just managed to prevent them from putting my leg in a cast. Chester came in and speculated about the advisability of a gunshot wound. He was joking, I think.

So I lay in that bare room for a month. I was in a considerable sweat most of the time because some of Connybear's acquaintances came by to visit me and I had to feign dizziness and loss of memory until I could get a few clues as to who they were and what their relationship with Connybear had been. Luckily no one came by asking for money – I was so tentative about my position I would have paid.

The orderly, whose name was Dagberry, put me in a lather when he came in beaming one night after I had been relieved of the head bandage.

'Good news for you, Connybear,' he said. 'Your sister is coming to visit you.'

'My sister!'

He studied a note in his hand. 'Yup. Miss Angela Connybear will arrive by rail from Seattle tomorrow.'

I laid aside the copy of R. Burton Deane's *Mounted Police Life in Canada*³ which Dagberry had fetched for me from the library when I'd said I wanted to read up on the traditions of the Force. Terribly dull stuff, but informative. 'I'm not sure I'm up to a family visit.'

'Of course you are. You're as fit as a fiddle. You're back to your old self.'

'Did you know my old self, Dagberry?'

'Well, no, I meant . . '

'You don't know what you're talking about!' I shouted.

'What's this? What's this?' Chester stood at the door. When he took off his stiff-brimmed hat and shook snow flakes from it I became aware of the cold air in the room. It had grown steadily colder over the past weeks and I had taken to wearing socks in bed. I'd grown a beard too. 'Got your bark back, Connybear? Pity you didn't have any bite when it counted.'

'Connybear's sister is coming to visit him, sir,' Dagberry said. 'But he doesn't seem to want to see her.'

'Nonsense.' Chester dissolved a snowflake on his hat with a gloved finger. 'You should see her, Connybear. It's going to be a long time before you see another friendly face. Your orders have come through. Is she pretty, your sister?'

'Mmm,' I said.

'Gaze upon her then. The female faces you are going to see for the next three years will be brown and flat and tattooed. D'you know what an Eskimo woman smells of, Connybear?'

'No, sir.'

'Fish fat, Connybear. *Old* fish fat.'

I sank back on the pillows and brooded. Dagberry tried to cheer me up by playing the harmonica but he stopped when I threw R. Burton Deane at him.

'Quit it,' I snarled, 'or you'll be playing it by farting into it. Know what I mean?'

Dagberry wiped the instrument on the sleeve of his white coat; among his other vices was tobacco chewing and he left a brown smear on the sleeve. He grinned evilly. 'You're a nasty man, Connybear. You don't deserve a nice sister like the one you got.'

'How d'you know she's nice?'

'Oh, someone told me he saw you with a blonde in Brady's tea-room one time. You said she was your sister. Prime womanhood, I'm told.'

'Is that so?'

'Yes. Maybe you don't remember after the blow to your head.'

'That's right.'

'Too bad. Well, she'll be here tonight and you can discuss your Ma 'n' Pa or whatever else concerns you. Would you like a shave or something, Connybear? I'm a right fine barber.'

I felt the short but strong beard I'd sprouted and considered the possibilities. A sister would be able to expose me for sure. On the other hand, a beard might confuse and delay her long enough for old Dick Browning to get his charm to work. Prime woman-hood, eh? That meant young or youngish. I never knew a woman yet who didn't respond well to a manly chap gallantly recovering from a wound. 'No, Dagberry, old fellow. No shave, thank you. D'you think you could arrange for me to be sitting up when she comes? Perhaps with my jacket on? I don't want to alarm her, you see.'

'I think I could manage that,' says Dagberry. 'I could even get a bit of a fire going in the corner there. Would you like that?'

'Great. Yeah, thanks.'

'What about a drop of something?'

'Well . . .'

'It'd cost you, mind. 'Gainst regulations and all.' He picked up the copy of *Mounted Police Life in Canada* and placed it reverently on the cabinet. I thought of the money in my jacket pocket. 'How long till she comes?'

'Not long. Half an hour maybe.'

'Get me in a chair an' get the fire going. Rustle up some sherry an' some brandy. I'll make it worth your while.'

'Henry!'

My first impulse was to turn around to see who else had come into the room. Here I am, seated by the fire in a clean shirt with my, or Connybear's, scarlet jacket draped around my broad shoulders. I was wearing the regulation pants with the broad stripe and non-regulation doeskin boots. Connybear and I were almost exactly of a size. Dick Browning, fine figure of a man and here's this handsome creature rushing into the room, all fur and satin and pearl buttons, hollering for Henry. Then it came to me: I hadn't heard Connybear's given name before.

She fluttered across the room and practically flung herself into my lap. I had to wrap my arms around her to keep my balance and then her perfume hit me like a wave. It had been so long since I'd held a woman. I couldn't stop myself – I was nuzzling into her, moving my hand up to her breast and searching for her lips before the door was closed behind her. She was just as enthusiastic; I felt her hand on my thigh and it wasn't up around the near. The lust was rising in me but I managed to hold it back. I grabbed her fine, strong shoulders and pushed her away.

'Here, hold on, Angela. This won't do!'

'Why? What's wrong, darling. Don't you love me any more?' She brushed my hands from her shoulders and thrust forward. Her hand was well at work now, stroking and pumping and her tongue was probing my ear.

'Well, of course. You're my dearest sister. Always liked you best . . .'

'Sister, my ass. C'mon, Hank, don't tell me you've lost your pistol. Oh!' She suddenly pushed back and looked at me. 'You weren't wounded there, were you. Oh, no!'

'No, nothing like that,' I said quickly. 'Just a tap on the head. I'm fine.' I was, too – her perfume and the soft warmth of her body were sending the messages racing through me and I was responding. She felt it and laughed.

'Same old Hank. You randy devil. Well, I paid off the orderly. Let's get to bed.'

'Er . . .'

'What is it now?' She stood and stripped off her coat. Under it I saw a strapping woman, five foot eight if an inch with a lush body, a round face and a mass of tumbling brown hair. She was made up to look twenty but was probably closer to thirty. My time in Hollywood had made me an expert on such matters. But her big white teeth and red lips were all her own. Her hands were working at her buttons and the bodice of her grey silk dress was coming open to reveal white lace and pink flesh.

I stood up and my jacket fell away. She stopped unbuttoning and came across to rub her hands over the hair on my chest.

'Oh, my,' she breathed. 'Oh, my.'

'Er, Angela. I took this knock on the head you see, an' I forget things a bit. You're, er . . . you're not my sister?'

She undid my belt. 'No, and I'm not your cousin or any other kind of kin that I know of. I don't think I'd care anyway. If'n you don't get over to this here bed I'll go call that orderly instead.'

That was enough for me. I kicked over the chair, picked her up and carried her to the bed. We clawed at each other's clothes, gasping and snorting, and the more her ripe, pink flesh came into view the more heated I got. There were a few odd garments still hanging around, like one of my doeskin boots and a black silk ribbon she wore around her throat, but we had the essentials unencumbered and fitted together in no time. We pounded away fit to break the bed and, sitting here more than fifty years and God knows how many women later, I really can't recall another female with the hip and buttock control of 'Klondike' Angie Jones.

That was her name as I discovered later as we lay in the sheets. The sister business was all my eye, something Connybear had dreamed up to get him out of a fix with another woman. Angie had played along with it for fun. Of course, she tumbled to me within seconds of our joining. You can't fool a woman about a thing like that. I felt a momentary stiffening of her body in surprise before she went into one of her monumental plunges, but it was only after that she wanted to talk about it.

'You ain't Hank Connybear.' She bit the lobe of my ear.

'Ouch. No, but for Christ sake don't tell anyone.'

'You're alike as twins. What's going on?'

'You're not complaining, are you?' I gave one of her big firm breasts a squeeze.

'No, I ain't,' she giggled. 'Not that Hank isn't a pretty fair man in the sack. But you . . .'

A more modest man might have admitted that he'd been sex-starved for a couple of months, but modesty was never my long suit and in any case I was going to have to play it cautious with Angie if I didn't want to be facing those gun-running charges or worse. I drew in a breath, stretched my legs and started in again. Fortunately the flesh was willing and I had her lying back and gasping by the time I'd finished.

'It's a long story,' I began.

There was a tap at the door and Dagberry strolled in carrying a tray which he put down on the hearth in front of the fire. He righted the chair and left without saying a word.

Angie and I wrapped ourselves in blankets and squatted by the fire. I was ravenous. I wolfed down the sliced meat and cheese and biscuits the orderly had brought and drank three quick sherries before taking a large brandy and soda at a slower pace. Angie ate heartily too, but contented herself with the sherry in small, ladylike sips. I told her my story, suitably edited, and she was gratifyingly responsive in the good bits, like when I worked with Fairbanks on *Robin Hood*. I pumped her for information on Connybear but she had little to offer. When drunk he'd told her that he joined the

Canadian Mounted to escape from some trouble in the east but had only succeeded into getting into more trouble on the prairies. It didn't surprise her that he'd been up to mischief in the west.

'He's a mischief maker,' she said. 'No harm in him but he just can't stay out of trouble.'

'He robbed three men and stole my boat,' I grumbled.

'Didn't kill anyone, I bet.'

I put some more wood on the fire. I hadn't ever been really ill, more humiliated and frightened really, but now I felt in better fettle and realised that I was chafing at my confinement. There was a whole world outside even if this particular patch of it, seen through the window, looked grey and cold.

Angie sipped her sherry and poured another. 'You're just like him, you know. Just like all men. You haven't asked me for a word about my own self.'

'I'm sorry, love. Yes, now, how d'you fit into all this? Didn't ever mention a plan to do a flit did he, Connybear?'

'There you are! Still thinking of yourself.'

I got her calmed down, pushed a bit more sherry into her and tried not to yawn too widely while I heard the story of her life. I don't recall much of it – born in Georgia or was it Louisiana? Doesn't matter. She was a dancer when she could be and a saloon girl when she couldn't. She'd met Connybear in a saloon in Seattle and he'd written to her a couple of times.

She fished into her bag and pulled out a newspaper clipping: 'Mountie Hero Confronts Terrorists' ran the headline and the story was in the same vein.

'I came up here to see a hero,' she sniffed. Her nose was getting a little red and her blue eyes were watering. 'I didn't expect to find a fraud.'

'Ssh. We had fun, didn't we? I must give you something for your fare.'

'Well . . .'

'And we must meet again.'

'Oh, yes!'

'Trouble is, I'm going to be posted to Dawson City.'

'Dawson City! Why, that's . . . oh, thank you, kind sir.' I'd pressed five dollars into her hand. I gave her a kiss on the shoulder and slipped the blanket down a little. 'It's so far away, but I do hear there are some mighty lively saloons up there. Those gold miners, when they strike it rich, there ain't nothin' they won't do to . . . for a girl.'

'You might consider coming up there, love? It sure would be good to see a friendly face.'

'Face?' Angie said. 'Are you sure you mean face?' We had a good laugh at that; the blanket slipped down further and we took some time to say our farewells, there on the blankets in front of the fire.

CHAPTER FOUR

They weren't about to send me packing off to the north on my lonesome. Chester, although a dreadful ramrod to his inferiors and lickspittle to others, was a fair judge of men and I had no doubt he'd seen through me by the end of my first week in bed. Just let me out of Vancouver unescorted and I'd have been turning sharp right and heading for the Great Lakes by road, rail or whatever other means was to hand. Chester must have read my mind.

'You're in for a journey north, laddie,' he said when he had me, all togged out with my beard trimmed and my boots polished, in front of his desk.

'Sir,' I said.

'I wouldn't want you to be lonely so I'm sending Sergeant Fraser along with you. The Sergeant has business in Dawson. He'll not be staying but he'll be happy to accompany you.'

'No need, sir,' I said stiffly. 'I'm sure I can find my way. I'm an old hand in the Yukon, you know.'

Chester sniffed. 'So I believe. All the more reason for Fraser to go along. You might get over-confident of the trail and become lost. You'll report to Marine Dock 4, that's the Mounted Police dock, at 9 a.m. sharp, Connybear, and be damn glad you're not going to prison under guard.'

'That's hard, sir. I . . .'

'D'you want me to mount an enquiry into where you got the money to bribe Dagberry to let that Yankee whore visit you, eh?'

'She's a southerner, sir, an' . . .'

'Cut your insolence! You're a scoundrel, Connybear. I'd like to see you and that gangster Browning in a cell together, but since I can't, I'll do the next best thing with you.'

You'll wait a long time for that sight, thinks I.I saluted smartly and marched out of the office. By this time I'd been up and about for a day or two, quite long enough to see that life in the Mounties was not for me. If it wasn't up at dawn to parade around on foot or horse, it was law lectures and classes on Mountie traditions. The one bright spot had been a stint at the pistol firing range. I'd told the Sergeant in command of the troop I'd been temporarily assigned to that I needed some practice and wanted to be sure that the blow on the head hadn't made me gun shy.

'Gun shy!' he rumbled. He was overweight by at least a hundred pounds and he probably hadn't been on a horse in years. The only thing I'd ever seen him sitting on was a chair. 'That's a good one. Where'd you pick that up? Gun shy!'

It was on the tip of my tongue to say in Hollywood, but I managed to suppress it. I'd had a lot of trouble trying to talk like Connybear and behave like a Canadian when I'd only spent a few minutes with the man and hadn't been in the country more than a few weeks and most of that in bed. I'd drawn a few odd looks, but no comments. I just stroked my beard and signed for the .38 Long Colt[4]. This was a double action revolver with swing-out cylinders of a kind I'd seen but hadn't handled. I went to the indoor target range and blazed away happily for fifteen minutes at silhouettes, still and moving. The range supervisor complimented me afterwards.

'You've improved, Connybear.'

'Eh, how's that?'

'You were down here a few days before the . . . ah, break out. Don't you remember?'

'Er . . .' I touched my head and blinked.

'You couldn't hit a horse at arm's length. That knock on the head must've done something to your eyesight and balance.'

'Ha, ha. Could be,' I said.

Apart from nasty moments like that and the odd difficulty with the daily drill, such as not saluting with a gloved hand unless on horseback, I managed pretty well. Connybear had left his kit behind so I had the opportunity to study his signature and operate his savings account after drawing my pay. Miserably small it was, though; I don't blame him a bit for deserting. Still, it was something to add to what I had left of the hundred dollars. This made a fair sum for those days and I felt pretty confident that I'd be able to elude Sergeant Fraser, jump ship somewhere, and buy myself some distance in another direction. Still, I didn't know the price of things in Canada and my experience is that newcomers to a country get fleeced from breakfast to supper. Dagberry came to see me an hour or so before I was due to report to Fraser. (I'd had very little time to look around Vancouver so I'd allowed much too much time for this move – the wharves were a short distance from the barracks.)

'Hello, Connybear,' Dagberry says, all breezy.

'Dagberry,' I said curtly. I knew he'd polished off the brandy and sherry himself after I'd paid through the nose for it; besides, he smelled of the infirmary.

'I . . . ah . . . double up as the post's medical records keeper, Connybear. Did you know that?'

I shook my head. I knew something bad was coming. You can always tell a blackmailer by the look in his eye. I should know, I've laid the arm on enough people myself in my time. Force of circumstance, of course.

Dagberry smiled and pretended to study the top of my head. I was sitting down on my bunk putting some last touches to my kit. 'Yes. Now, it's a matter of your war service, Connybear. France and all that.'

'Sure. I served in France.' That was true enough; I was mostly ducking for cover and looking for messenger jobs that would carry me backwards rather than forwards, but I felt on pretty safe ground with France.

Dagberry looked at the ceiling. 'Sergeant Henry Connybear,' he recited, 'Seventh Battalion, Canadian Corps, saw action at the Somme, Chateau Terry . . .'

'Chateau Thierry,' I corrected.

'Yup. Wounded in action, leg and shoulder.'

'Oh. Well, I had the best of . . .'

'I've seen you the way your Mama saw you, mister, front and back, and the worst wound you ever had was when you nicked yourself shaving.'

I stood up. I towered over Dagberry by nearly a foot and as I rose I pulled Connybear's hunting knife from the bag. Dagberry went even paler than he was naturally, but greed overcame fear. 'You . . . you won't do anythin', not here.'

'Nothin' fatal, maybe. What's on your mind?'

'The balance of the money. I make it seventy-five dollars near enough. That buys my silence.'

'For how long?'

'For good and all. I'm not greedy.'

I thought about it. I thought about running the knife through him too, and putting him under the bunk and catching the boat north. But drastic action has never been my metier. 'Tell you what I'll do, Dagberry. I'll give you fifty dollars.'

'That ain't much.'

'Neither are you. Fifty, an' you give me the medical sheet.'

'Hell, no. I can't . . .'

I brought the knife up and put the point under his chin. 'I can't take the risk of leaving you here behind to do as you like. What if you take a drop too much? I know you like it. No, I need something that points to you.'

'Your voice sounds funny. Who the hell are you?'

I realised that the native Australian must have come through in my voice. I nicked his pimply neck with the blade and broadened the accent. 'Mate,' I said, 'you don't really want to know who I am. You just run along and get that bloody paper.'

Dagberry did it; he really didn't have much talent as a blackmailer. The transaction left me very short of funds and made me less confident which was a pity because confidence was something you needed plenty of in your dealings with Sergeant Martin Fraser. I arrived at the dock, shivering a bit inside my heavy greatcoat because the year was wearing on and it was getting cold. I had the regulation kitbag full of the regulation stuff as well as a bedroll and two bottles of brandy to juggle. The day was gloomy with a wind coming off the water that smelled of fish. I saw a tall figure leaning against the rail at the end of the dock and I lumbered towards it. As I got closer I could see that tall wasn't the word. Fraser must have stood six feet six in his stockings and now he was in boots with his hat on. He straightened up and let his long jaw jut out. His eyes were a hard, pale grey and he had a long thin nose just made for looking down. A pipe held between clenched teeth made his expression grim and unforgiving. He looked like a Presbyterian minister, dressed up in funny clothes and stretched a foot or more.

'You'll be Connybear?' He managed to put a good-sized sneer into it.

'Yes, Sergeant.'

'Drop your gear and salute, so we'll be off on the right footing.'

I did it. The bottles clinked and Fraser held out a white gloved hand. 'Give it here.'

I handed one of the bottles to him and he threw it over his shoulder into the water without even glancing at it.

'I'm a teetotaller,' he said. 'There's our craft; time to board.'

The *Barraclough* was a cumbersome-looking thing – a forty-foot steam launch, built broad and solid. Later I was to find out the reason for this unstylish construction. Fraser and I carried our traps down a ladder onto the aft deck and got directions to our cabin from a seaman whose whole face seemed to be covered by beard. The cabin was small but clean. Fraser took the bottom bunk so he could allow his long legs to protrude; a locker confined the top bunk to about six feet in length which meant I'd have to curl up a bit. We stowed our gear away, me taking care to keep the brandy out of sight, and Fraser ensuring that I saw his Long Colt and handcuffs. Connybear, of course, had taken his sidearm with him and I hadn't thought to apply for a re-issue. I regretted that now, along with a lot of other things.

Fraser was a taciturn individual. I tried to make conversation about this and that but he contented himself with the briefest of replies. He had a knack of making you feel a fool while you were talking, a useful trick for a man who didn't like to talk himself and really didn't have much to say. He lay on his bunk and perused a couple of books; one was on fishing, the other was Henry Hartman's *The Eskimos: Their Habits and Habitat*. I gazed out of the porthole at the greasy, grey water. The *Barraclough* was wallowing a little, even firmly tied to the dock as she was. There's almost nothing more boring than being in an immobile boat (unless it's being with an immobile woman) and I forced myself back into human contact.

'Interested in the Eskimos, are you, Sergeant?' I said to the image on the front of the book Fraser was holding. It showed a moon-faced man, furred to the eyebrows, examining the point of a wicked-looking barbed spear.

'Yes,' Fraser said. He must have been *really* interested because he added, 'I've made a study of the primitive races of Canada – Indians and Eskimos.'

I vaguely remembered seeing some photographs of specimens of both in a London illustrated magazine. 'Oh, yes,' I said idly, 'both the same thing, surely.'

'Not at all!' I had his attention now and no mistake. He put the book down and puffed vigorously on his pipe. 'It's a common misconception to think that the Indians and the Eskimos are the same people.'

'Look alike,' I said.

'Nonsense.' Puff, puff. 'There are important physiological differences'. More significant though are the languages . . .'

I was well and truly bored by this time and sorry I'd ever got him started. But at least something was happening apart from the movement of the ship and the occasional bird cry from overhead. He was still expounding on the Nootkas and Punucks, making gutteral sucking and blowing noises and doing odd things with his tongue, when the *Barraclough* gave a lurch and shudder and got underway. The only English words I caught in Fraser's lecture at that point were 'Arctic Sea'. A shiver ran through me as I registered them. Truth is, I've never been too fond of the cold and it struck me for the first time that I was heading for a solid dose of it. But geography was never my strong point back at Dudleigh Grammar; I recalled a lot of dull stuff about mountains and valleys and not much else. I had only the roughest idea of the shape of Canada and not a clue about the latitudes involved. I imagined that Dawson City might be something like Hobart in Tasmania – damn cold in winter but pleasant enough in the summer months which, after all, were almost upon us.

'Very interesting, Sergeant,' I said. 'I haven't exactly been to Dawson City. In the neighbourhood only, you understand. What sort of a place is it?'

Fraser sucked on his pipe; he looked irritated at being interrupted in his clucking. 'Well, you know the Yukon?'

'Mm,' I said.

'You know what this vessel's business is?'

'Not exactly.'

'You're a bigger fool than I took you for, then. The *Barraclough*'s a government supply ship, carries equipment for government

facilities up the coast, also the mail. We'll be putting in to drop
mail and goods all the distance to Skagway.'

'What then?'

'We'll go by the Chilkoot Pass and then on to Whitehorse.'

'Travelling how?'

'By railway, narrow gauge. Then from Whitehorse to Dawson.'

'Still by rail?'

'No, by river steamer – downstream on the Yukon River to
Dawson City. That's Touchown territory of course.'

'Ah, yes. Well, that'll put us pretty far north, eh? Pretty chilly?'

Fraser refilled his pipe, lit it and took up his fishing book. 'I
wouldn't say that, Connybear.' He let go a thin, wintery smile as
he made the only thing approaching a joke I ever heard from him.
'You'll be almost two hundred miles on the warm side of the Arctic
Circle.'

CHAPTER FIVE

As a sea cruise it left a lot to be desired. The *Barraclough* was slow and steady; the condition of the wind and water didn't seem to make any difference to her. Fraser snorted when I remarked one day on her stout construction. We were standing on deck catching some faint sunlight.

'That's for the floes and pack ice when we get to the north.' Smoke streaming from his pipe was snatched away by a keen wind.

'Not at this time of year, surely?'

'Depends on the thaw and the currents. It can happen any time. I've seen ships crushed to matchwood.'

That was Fraser all over, not a cheerful conversationalist. I'd tried to get him to play cards, hoping to win a little cash, but he refused. He'd served all over Canada from the far north to the central plains and his knowledge of the country was vast. He was just the chap to fill me in on things I'd need to know when I made my move, but he seemed to avoid every practical subject. The only matter he'd open up on was those damn Indians. He'd growl and cluck away in their heathen tongues and despite myself I learnt a smattering of Shimshan, a dialect spoken, according to Fraser, over a good deal of the north-west.

The sailors weren't much better. Taciturn Scots and dour Norwegians most of them. (A second generation American *is* an American, with all the loud-mouthed uppishness that entails; not so with Canadians who seem to still bear the characteristics of their countries of origin.) Anyway, these silent salts got quieter and more contented the further north we went and the colder it became.

I got a bit more change out of Reuben Dawes. He said he'd been born aboard ship when his parents emigrated to the United States from England, and he boasted that he only put a foot ashore to drink. He was a stocky, weatherbeaten character, not much older than me but work had aged him. His back was bent and his body was a mass of rope scars, particularly his hands and forearms. But he sang sea shanties to his own banjo playing, played cards like a demon and was cheerful at least fifty per cent of the time.

As Fraser had said it would, the *Barraclough* was putting in at coastal towns and hamlets up the coast, dropping and collecting mail and landing cargo. It was infernally dull; I even tried to relieve the boredom early in the voyage by helping with the stevedoring. A good deal later in my life, when I'd fallen on hard times, I worked in Argentina in a meat chilling plant – the experiences, hauling cargo in chilling winds and frosty spray and shifting beef carcasses along icy floors, were roughly similar. I soon withdrew my labour and spent the time looking at the sea and sneaking off to nip at my brandy bottle.

When the brandy had gone and the cigarettes were running low I got the opportunity to put Reuben's boast that he only went ashore to drink to the test. We landed at a godforsaken place about halfway up the coast. I can't recall the name but it sounded more Russian than anything else. The village was on a small island – one of the thousands of desperate, barren rocks that go by the name of islands in those parts. There was no possibility of doing a bunk from it so Fraser was happy to stay in the cabin practising his Aleutian while Reuben and I went ashore.

There was a pale sun shining and some wildflowers were clinging to the bare rocky faces of the island's hills. Reuben and I wore coats, gloves and balaclavas and still the wind seemed to penetrate and freeze the flesh.

'Jesus,' I said, 'what in God's name goes on here?'

We tramped along the dock and went through a slipway towards a muddy road. 'Timber mostly,' Reuben said, 'also they catch and freeze fish.'

'The freezing part must be easy.' We slogged along the road through an icy mush deeply imprinted by wheel tracks and horse's hooves.

'Keep your head down, Hank. You'll freeze your eyeballs looking up at the hilltops like that. Why're you doing it, anyway?'

'I was thinking that the only way out of here would be by airplane. Up and over.' I pointed to the high grey clouds.

'I thought you had the look of a scarperer. We're nearly to the inn. We can have a few jars and you can tell me about it.'

The inn, a rough log cabin with mud-caulked and whitewashed walls and floors and furniture that looked to have been hacked out of the trees by hand, had just opened for the day. Reuben bought a bottle of whisky and took two enamel mugs off hooks on the wall. After a toast to drinking itself, I told Reuben Dawes the greatest pack of lies I'd produced up to that time. I'd been tricked into rejoining the Mounties, I said, by a promise of promotion that wasn't forthcoming. I was a victim, I said, of internal politics and rivalry. Talk of this kind is music to a sailor's ears. My time aboard the *Sternwood*, when I worked my passage from Australia to the United States[6], had taught me that sailors bicker and squabble and form and break alliances like school kids. Reuben lapped it up. I went on to say that I had a sweetheart in Montreal and couldn't bear to be separated from her by the length and breadth of Canada. Warming to the theme, and warmed by some good Canadian whisky (the Canadians didn't have Prohibition, which was the only good thing I'd found about the place so far), I told Reuben about Cameron MacKnight. As it happened, this was the name of my father-in-law, who, I fervently hoped, was dead by now back in Australia, but in my fireside chat with Reuben he became an unscrupulous lawyer who was trying to marry my Ellen and take her inheritance. God knows where I got this sort of rubbish from, possibly from the movies, or maybe from hearing my sisters talk about the sloppy novels they read one after another. Reuben, who must have had a damaged liver because he had no capacity for strong drink at all, loved it.

'A terrible thing,' he said, 'to pluck a young man from his loved one. I loved a girl once myself, I . . .'

'Yes, yes,' I said, 'but the point is, how do I get away from the bloody place?'

'Eh?' Reuben was growing confused by this time. There were about twenty men in the place, rough fellows all – beards, slouch hats, woollen caps, greatcoats and half-ton boots. The bar was a long slab of pine atop two barrels and the drinkers leaned against it and the walls. There were two trestle tables with benches pulled up to them and Reuben and I, as the first customers, had the choice spot – two straight-backed chairs by the fire. Everyone was smoking; Reuben and I were rolling cigarettes with his rough sailor's shag and cigars and pipes were contributing to the fug. Occasionally a man leaned across us and spat tobacco juice into the fire. It was a steamy, manly atmosphere, very conducive to getting blind drunk, and Reuben was well on the way.

'This Fraser bastard is watching me like a hawk,' I said.

'Bloody Scot,' Reuben slurred, 'all bastards . . .'

'So I can't see how I can get clear before Dawson City.'

'Fine place, for a coupla weeks a year . . .'

'You've been there? I thought you never went ashore?'

'Not 'zackly ashore. Worked on the river steamers for a while. Yukon River.'

'Ah.' I said.

Reuben wagged his finger at me. 'Know what you're thinkin', Hank. Forget it, my son. The Mounties control that bloody river, length 'n' bloody breadth of it. It's the way the thieves an' murderers come in 'n' out, see?'

'Thieves and murderers? Way up there?'

'Believe it. Ever hear of Soapy Smith?'[7]

'Don't recall the name. Steady, Reuben, don't you think you've had enough?'

'Gotta finish the bottle. Can't take it on board. Just a drop. Well, ol' Soapy Smith, worst bloody cut-throat in North America. Usta rob people, strip 'em of everythin', leave 'em to die in the snow – women, babies . . .'

'Christ! Where was this?'

'Up where you goin' – Skagway, th' Yukon.'

'When?'

'Ah, well, must've been before the war. 'Bout 1890 . . . somethin'.'

'Christ, Reuben. We still had bushrangers back in Australia then. Wild blackfellows too, they . . .'

'Eh? What's that?' He squinted at me from bloodshot eyes.

'Er . . . nothing. Well, you were saying about the river. Must be other ways of travelling on it apart from steamers. It sounds like the smart way to go.'

'Oh, it's the smart way all right. You c'n go on the rivers clear to Edmonton, pick up the Canadian Pacific. Take you all the way to Montreal an' your sweet Ellen.'

'Who? Oh, yes.' I was getting a bit stewed myself by this time. 'Must be boats for sale somewhere.'

Reuben let out a cackle of laughter. Then he lit his cigarette and burnt his fingers. He swore and dropped the butt in the fire. He looked angry now and I wondered whether he was a fighting drunk. He glared belligerently around the room for a second but the light went out of his eyes and he grinned. 'Roll us 'nother smoke, Hank. Yes, there's other ways of travellin' on the river. Look over there.'

'At what?' I was having trouble rolling the tobacco and also focussing on the group of men by the bar.

'You can go down th' river on logs. They let these logs go and they *rush* along, go for miles . . .' He demonstrated with a sweep of his hand that jolted the elbow of a big, black-bearded man standing behind him. Whisky spilled and flared as drops hit the flames.

'Easy, you,' the man growled.

'Easy, nothing!' Reuben got out of his chair and drew himself up to his full five foot six inches. He threw a punch at the beard which ended at about eye level for him, that is to say, halfway down its owner's chest. The punch was caught in a giant fist and Reuben was shoved across the room. He was so drunk that he tried to stay on his feet which meant that he went backwards like a cyclist in reverse and cannoned into the knot of men by the bar. Drinks were spilled and curses were shouted. Another oversized individual took reprisals for losing his whisky by pounding Reuben's head into the bar. This knocked over other mugs and brought more shouts and punches. I tried to sneak out the door but I was tripped by a man careering wildly back from the fray. He grabbed me for support and lurched back into the melee carrying me with him. I took a blow to the chest that would have felled a mule and I dropped to the floor thinking it might be safer there. It wasn't: boots beat a tattoo around my head and I had to scramble across the rough planks, picking up splinters along the way and trying to keep my hands out of the way of the hobnails and metal toecaps.

I stood to make a bolt for the door and was knocked over by a backhander. Confused, I stood up in the middle of a fist fight between two hairy, smelly monsters who probably spent their work-ing hours on a crosscut saw. I went down again and found Reuben with his face in the slops.

'We have to get out of here.'

'That's right, bastards! Out!'

For a moment I thought Reuben had collected his wits and somehow taken on the strength of ten, but it was a bald-headed ox of a chap, four feet around the middle if an inch, who grabbed both our collars and dragged us to the door. Reuben struggled but I went willingly.

Our conductor pinned Reuben to the wall with his shoulder while he heaved open the door. He slung me through it like a wheat lumper tossing a bag onto a dray.[8] From the porch, flat on my back, I saw him get his balance and grab Reuben by the collar and belt. The next I knew my shipmate had landed on top of me. I smelt his whisky breath in my face and felt the wind go out of me in a rush.

I lay still. Reuben lay still. Then he stirred and rolled off. He sat and felt along his limbs, methodically, one by one.

'What the hell are you doing?' I gasped.

''M checkin' for breaks. Did you see 'im?'

'Who?'

'Feller who chucked us out.'

'Of course I saw him. Nearly broke my neck.'

Reuben hoisted himself to his feet with the aid of the porch post. 'But did you get a good look at 'im? At 'is leg?'

'No . . . wait.' I thought back. There was still a lot of noise coming from inside, but after one more shattering crash as if the pine bar had been splintered from end to end, it subsided. I tried to picture the man who'd tosssed me around like a toy. 'Yes,' I said, 'there was something funny about his leg. The way he got his balance . . .'

'That's it!' Reuben cackled. 'What I was tryin' to tell you before that black-bearded bastard clobbered me. He was a lumberjack before he was a barman. He's got a peg leg. He went down the river on the logs, see. An' those logs nipped his leg off neat as scissors. That's the Yukon River for you, boy.'

'Thanks, Reuben,' I said.

CHAPTER SIX

Back on the *Barraclough* Fraser observed my scratches and bruises
without comment. Stripped to his vest and shorts he did exer-
cises on the deck, and he regularly scrubbed himself down with
hard soap and buckets of sea water. He used a cut-throat razor to
shave himself to a pink, baby smoothness. Fit and clean, he tied
lures for trout and went on with his studies of Indian and Eskimo
ethnology for relaxation. I moped around the ship vainly trying
to get up card games; I let my beard and hair grow and wasn't
particular about washing. I lounged around with Reuben in his
free time, learnt a few chords on the banjo and kept my passable
baritone in trim. [At this point in the tape Browning breaks off
and sings a few lines of 'Oh Susannah'. His voice is cracked and
old, making it hard to tell what the quality of the young man's
voice might have been. It is possible that he could have carried a
tune passably. Ed.]

Fraser's opinion of me, therefore, worsened, if that was possible,
and Reuben wasn't the most comfortable companion either. My slip
about the bushrangers and blackfellows had lodged in his drunken
brain and stuck. Thereafter he persisted in trying to catch me out.
He'd tinkle away at an Irish ballad and then turn it into 'The Wild
Colonial Boy' or 'Brave Ben Hall' or some other ditty that I'd known
since I could talk, and watch for my reaction. I think I kept a poker
face. Reuben had been to Australia, you see, and he could mispro-
nounce place names like Mel-born and tell me how Tulkeroo had

won the Cup[9] in 1908 and wait for me to correct him. I didn't bite but it was hard going sometimes.

What with these irritations and the boredom of shipboard life I was almost looking forward to arriving in Skagway. The ship made slow progress due to the frequent calls, some of which had to be made by dinghy because there were no jetties. We were in what was called the 'inside passage' and the water was protected from the ocean winds and relatively calm, although there were treacherous rocks and shoals. Fraser, of course, was up on deck most of the time taking an active interest in the bird life. Myself, I would have been more interested in a cow, preferably cut into steaks – I was getting damn sick of fish and rice.

A day out of Skagway I happened to be up on deck with Fraser. Even he was rugged up in a skin coat with fur hood. The wind off the land seemed to freeze my beard.

'Uncommon cold for this time of year,' Fraser said. 'See the ice in the river mouth?'

We were in a bay which was fed by a wide stream from the coastal mountains. There was snow on the middle reaches and I could see patches of whitish blue in the muddy river water.

'Is that the pack ice you were talking about? Are we going to get stuck?'

Just then I felt a bump and I rushed to the rail. The *Barraclough* had nudged a piece of floating ice and sent it spinning away. Fraser joined me at the rail.

'No,' he said contemptuously. 'We're not going to get stuck. Might have to do a bit more of that off Skagway but that's all. Going to be a cold one though.'

'Dawson City's been around for a long time, hasn't it?' I lit a cigarette and kept it cupped in my hand. 'Must be reasonably comfortable. This isn't the gold rush days, eh, Sergeant?'

He shot me a sideways glance. 'No, Dawson's not too bad. Rough but comfortable enough. But where you're going it's a different story.'

'What d'you mean?' I yelped. 'Where *am* I going?'

Fraser puffed contentedly on his pipe. 'I took the liberty of reading your order papers, just in case they got lost and I had to give a verbal report to the Comptroller, you understand. Seems you volunteered for Arctic duty. You specifically asked for a post on the Mackenzie. That's inside the Circle.'

'It's a lie!' I shouted. 'I didn't volunteer for anything. I hate the cold. I've never been south of Phillip[10]. . .'

Fraser took his pipe out of his mouth and turned his hooded head to look at me. 'There's something odd about you, Connybear. Something that doesn't fit. I don't know what it is but you're going to the right place. The north'll make a man of you.'

'If it doesn't make me an iceberg.'

He nodded. 'It's dangerous, to be sure. It'll be up to you.'

There's not much to say about Skagway, Alaska. Beautiful setting, of course, in a sort of fjord with towering peaks around, that looked faintly green up in the pale sky. But I've known shithole places look lovely when things were going good and sunny paradises seem like hell when my stocks were low. Low was the word for me when I hit Skagway so I wasn't much taken by the natural beauty. It was a busy place in the gold rush days with riff raff from all over the world pouring in. Had its share of sin in those days, I daresay but it was pretty bloody quiet in late 1922. I remember that insurance came into my mind when I looked at the buildings flanking the wide, roughly paved Front Street. They were all made of timber, you see, or nearly all. A good torching and someone could've made a handsome pile. I haven't been back since those times, needless to say, but I suppose it hasn't changed much unless it's become a tourist attraction. God knows why anyone would want to freeze his ass off in a log cabin voluntarily but tourists will do anything.

In fact, there were a couple of men you could call kind of tourists in the place when we arrived in the *Barraclough*. I ran into them in the hotel where Fraser and I put up for the night before catching the train over the Chilkoot Pass. Fraser and I checked into our rooms. He went to discuss police business with the representatives of law and order in Skagway and I had a farewell drink with Reuben Dawes in the bar. Although it was an American possession, Alaska wasn't yet a state and wasn't subject to the Volstead Act. I doubt if they could've enforced such insanity up there. Reuben and I breasted the bar, ordered whiskies and found ourselves standing next to two men who were drinking rum. Both were solid, well-fleshed characters aged fifty or more. Their clothes and shoes were expensive, they were smoking dollar cigars and had rings on their fingers and watches worth hundreds but their hands bore the marks of rough work and their voices were those of men who'd rather spit than use a handkerchief.

'Old town ain't what it used to be, Ollie,' says one of them, knocking back a couple of ounces of rum.

'Here's cheers, Hank,' Reuben said. He drank off his whisky and slammed the glass down. 'Your shout,' he said, watching me out of the corner of his eye.

'Blast me,' says the other rum drinker, who, I noticed, was dark-skinned with a slightly Oriental look about him. He had a white moustache but it was very sparse compared to his companion's luxuriant pepper and salt growth. 'I ain't heard that since we used to drink with Kangaroo Pete in the Klondike in '97. Remember, Charley. He'd put his glass down, just like that and say, "Whose shout?"' Reuben looked sourly at them while they pounded each other's shoulders and laughed. I took a quiet sip of my drink and sat pat.

'I'm sorry, partner,' the one called Ollie said. 'Me 'n' Charley here's reliving old times. Didn't mean to be rude or nothing. You an Aussie?'

'No,' Reuben said.

'Didn't think so,' says Charley, 'mostly big, raw-boned guys, more like your friend there.' He tipped his hat in my direction. 'If you'll excuse me saying so, mister.'

I nodded and smiled.

'I'll get back to the ship, Hank.' Reuben and I shook hands. We'd had some good times but I wasn't sorry to see him go. Operating under an alias is bad enough without having someone around with a twitching nose.

'Well,' Charley says, 'my shout.' That set them laughing again and this time I joined in. I was short of money and this pair looked as if they could go on shouting all night.

We settled in at a table and after a few more rounds I had their stories. Oliver Fisher and Charley Moon were gold prospectors who'd struck it rich in the Klondike in 1896 and '97. To hear them tell it they'd grubbed the gold out of the frozen earth with their bare hands. They both made big strikes on the same creek, worked them night and day, fought off claim jumpers and bandits, and left the territory with enough money to last them the rest of their lives.

'Never thought I'd come back,' Ollie said. 'Got me a ranch in Wyoming, fine cattle, good wife. Never put a spade in the ground again 'cept to dig a fence post and I don't much care to do that.'

'What brought you back then?' I asked politely.

'This old varmit came driving through in his goddamned Buick. We'd lost touch, see? See how he's fatter 'n me? Well, he's richer too.'

They laughed some more and I bought a round – my first.

'Spit in your eye,' Charley said. 'Yeah, I got rich. Got in on some oil in Oklahoma. They tried to cheat me out of it of course, but an old Yukon man don't cheat easy.'

'Why d'you say of course?'

'Ain't you had a good look at me, Hank? Can't you see I don't come from London, England nor Dublin, Ireland?'

'Well . . .'

He bent his head closer to mine over the table. 'Part Indian,' he said. 'Han, from around where Dawson City now stands. 'Course, I don't go round in beads and make a war dance 'bout it.'

'Charley left these parts as a kid and went to sea,' Ollie said. 'Came back after the gold and I'm here to tell you what he knew about this country as an Indian paid him off a hundred times as a white man lookin' for gold.'

'I can see how it would,' I said. 'And now you're back in your happy hunting ground.' I could've bitten my tongue out as soon as I'd said it but, fortunately, Charley and Ollie were at the merry stage and they found it funny. When the merriment had died down they asked me about myself and I gave them the prepared story. They shook their heads at the mention of the Mackenzie River.

'Never been there,' Charley said, 'and wouldn't want to.' He said something in the clucking kind of language Fraser had been spouting on ship and I was surprised to find that I caught the gist of it.

'Raw meat eaters,' I said.

Charley looked surprised. 'Hey, that's right. That's what the Injuns call the Eskimos. You speak Kutchin?'

'Not really. Few words.'

'That could be useful,' Charley said.

'How d'you mean?'

The two men exchanged glances. Both nodded and the heads came in over the table again. 'Ollie an' me, we seen thousands of men come into this territory. Right, Ollie?'

Ollie nodded. 'And we've seen 'em in boxes going into the ground that was so cold they had to blast to make graves.'

'Jesus,' I said, 'what's your point?'

'You get so's you can judge a man. Whether he's fit for this place or not. Was you in the war?' Ollie sipped his rum; it must have been his tenth but he didn't seem to be affected by them.

'Yes.'

'Maybe you know what I mean, then. I heard old sodjers say you can tell when a man's not goin' to come through the action. Something about him. That right?'

I tried to remember. I'd shut out a lot of the memories of those dreadful days and nights in France with the artillery booming and the ground shaking and the night sky lit up momentarily by flashes brighter than the moon and stars. I could remember hands trembling on rifle stocks on freezing nights and pale faces dripping with sweat despite the cold. 'I know what you mean,' I said.

'No offence, Hank,' Charley Moon said. 'But you got that look to me. If'n you go to the Mackenzie your time is up.'

Ollie clapped his hands. 'Jesus, Charley, this is no way to be talking. That could all be crap. We haven't been here in a long, long time. They've got modern conveniences now – roads, oil stoves, airplanes, for Chrissake. This ain't the nineteenth goddamn century.'

Hunched over his drink, his dark hair falling in his face, Charley Moon suddenly looked very like an Indian. 'The Circle don't know it's the twentieth century,' he said.

'Let's eat,' Ollie said. 'C'mon, Hank, you're our guest.'

I smiled, drained my drink and tried to shake off the gloom. *Indians and Aborigines*, I thought. *Both the same, all wailing about sticks and stones and death.* 'Thank you, gentlemen,' I said, 'I'll be honoured to join you. Perhaps you'd like to hear about some of my exploits in the Royal Northwest Mounted Police.'

We stood and moved towards the dining room. Charley put his arm around my shoulder and spoke in my ear. 'If you're a Mountie, I'm a Zulu. An' if you need some help so's you don't have to go to the Mackenzie maybe I'm your man. Me 'n' Ollie's goin' on to Dawson. You need help, come to me.'

'Why would you do that, Charley?'

He patted my shoulder. 'You remind me of Kangaroo Pete; the way you look, the way you move. Pete saved my life in a rockfall on the Yukon in '96.'

Fraser came into the bar and I introduced him to Ollie and Pete. He informed me that we'd be leaving at 8 a.m. the following morning and that I should prepare myself to be under orders in the district to which I was assigned. I didn't have the faintest idea what he meant and I was drunk. I clicked my heels and saluted. Fraser sniffed and marched away.

Ollie and Charley told Mountie jokes over dinner (steaks and fried potatoes as I recall), and we drank much more red wine than was good for us.

'Saw a list of Mountie casualties once,' Ollie said around a mouthful of potatoes. 'Know what killed most of 'em, Hank?'

I thought of my own brief period of service. 'Boredom?'

'Hah, that's a good 'un. No, not boredom nor getting shot by renegade Injuns either – 'scuse me, Charley.'

Charley Moon inclined his head gravely, the wine had got to him finally. 'You're talkin' 'bout a fine body of men, Ollie,' he said. 'I should know, coupla my sisters got raped by 'em.'

Ollie swallowed; put down his knife and fork and raised his glass. 'Biggest cause of Mountie death is drowning. Can you swim, Hank?'

'Yes,' I said.

'First Mountie I ever met who could swim,' Ollie muttered.

Charley Moon drank some wine and held his glass up to the light. 'Propose a toast to our fren' Hank. May he avoid boredom, Injuns and drownin'.'

I drank enthusiastically enough to that. I didn't know it then, but I was heading straight into a lot of the first and the second and damned close encounters with the third.

CHAPTER SEVEN

Nowadays if I was to wake up with the kind of head I had on that September morning in Skagway, Alaska, in 1922, I'd know just what to do. I'd have one of the girls make me up vodka and tomato juice with an egg beaten up in it and I'd snort just one short line of coke and put the drink down my throat fast. Then I'd climb into the hot tub and soak and bubble a while and after that I'd get Rosalie to give me a long, warm oil massage. By the time her arms got tired I'd have other work for her to do.

But I knew nothing then about how to look after my body. Fraser hauled me out of bed and I cursed him and threw up and got dressed and threw up again and finally steadied myself with a pull on a brandy bottle I'd somehow finished up with after a long, long night with Ollie Fisher and Charley Moon.

Fraser was eating breakfast when I joined him with my bag packed and my headache settled down to a steady beat.

'I thought I told you to get ready to be under orders,' he said.

I looked at the eggs and bacon on his plate and shuddered. 'I don't feel well.'

'I'm not surprised. You're going to have to cut that hair and trim that beard. God help you if you don't get it done before you report to the depot in Dawson.'

I had my own thoughts about that but I just nodded and considered the question of coffee. When I decided I could manage some I sat down. Fraser wiped his mouth and stood.

'What're you doing?' he said.

'Need some coffee,' I muttered.

'No time. Train goes on the hour. We'll just catch it, you've made us late as it is.'

Waiting for the train, stamping their feet against the cold, were a few dozen people bound for Dawson City. A couple looked like school teachers; there was one certain minister of religion and the rest were a mixed bunch of workers, merchants and railroad men. Fraser sat himself near a window, opened it a fraction and lit his pipe. I'd thought to stick with him and pump him for as much information about Mountie life in the north as I could but the smell of the pipe was too much for me. I dropped my bag and headed for the observation car. It occurred to me that I hadn't seen Ollie and Charley. The train was about to pull out when I saw them hurrying along the platform. For oldish, heavy men with hangovers they moved surprisingly fast. They saw me and gave a wave as they swung aboard.

The Whitehorse & Yukon line was narrow gauge and the train followed the winding Dyea River for a distance before it bucked and swayed and kicked its way up the Chilkoot Pass. The rail bed seemed mostly to have been cut through the rock, especially in the steeper parts; on the easier grades I could see signs of an earlier track but it must have been brutally hard going without an engine to push or pull. I stood on the half-enclosed platform feeling the wind cut through me. The air got colder the higher we climbed.

'Used to be a Maxim gun down there on the pass,' Ollie Fisher said. 'How do, Hank?'

'Howdy, Hank.' Charley Moon stepped through the door after Ollie.

'Mornin', gents,' I said. 'How's the heads?'

'Feels like I been down a sluice head first,' Ollie grunted. 'Remember the Maxim gun, Charley?'

'Sure do. They could swing it to traverse . . . oh, all they need to, I guess.'

'Maxim gun?' I said. 'What for?'

'Undesirables,' Ollie said. 'There was every kind of riff raff poured in here in those days. Wouldn't have been surprised to see people with two heads, there was every other kind. Some of'em real bad.'

'You mean like Soapy Smith?'

Charley spat onto the line rushing away below us. 'No, ol' Soapy, he weren't too bad. He was a gentleman compared to some.'

The line zigzagged and the three of us had to hang on to each other and the handrails to stay upright. 'You knew Soapy Smith?' I asked.

'Manner of speaking,' Ollie said. 'Let's get inside. I got a bottle in my bag and I'm starved with the cold out here.'

We went back into the coach and settled down in a compartment without the reverend or the school teachers or any women of whom there were a couple on the train. We all began to feel better after a few nips on the bottle and after I got the first few lungsful of smoke down I felt fine as only a healthy twenty-five-year-old can. Just idly I asked Charley why it had taken so long for him to revisit the scene of his big strike. He glanced uneasily at Ollie.

'What sort of question's that?' Ollie said.

'Oh, nothing. Just curious.'

'We told you, Hank,' Charley said softly, 'we was in business in our different ways. Takes time to build a stake into something solid.'

Ollie coughed on his cigar and I looked out the window. The story seemed to have changed somewhat overnight but who was I to press people for accuracy and consistency. I was an Australian-born deserter turned movie actor and rum-runner masquerading as a member of the Northwest Mounted Police. If a Chinaman wanted to call himself Angus McTavish of Glasgow it was fine with me.

Fraser wandered through on his way to the observation platform, possibly to study birdlife but more likely to keep an eye on me. A curt nod was all I got from him and all I gave.

'He's a sharp one,' Charley said. 'He goin' to Mackenzie too?'

'Don't remind me,' I shivered involuntarily as I spoke. 'No, he's got business in Dawson, then he's heading back.'

'Good. You wouldn't have a chance of getting clear with him around. He's got the eye.'

'What eye?'

'Man-huntin' eye. He'd enjoy it.'

'Shit, Charley, this thing slows down on the bends. Why don't I just jump out and take my chances.'

'Then you'd just be between the police in Skagway and the Mounties in Whitehorse. Not smart. Be patient. You might get to stay in Dawson where it ain't so bad.'

'And if not?'

'You'll get your chance. Why I remember when Ollie and me were . . .'

'Yes?'

'Don't matter. Look, we're crossing back into Canada.'

We were at the top of the pass. The train stopped briefly but if there were any formalities about crossing from Alaska into Canada I don't remember them. The stop seemed to be to allow some of the passengers to take photographs. I got down to stretch my legs and stepped back almost straight away. The air was colder than I'd ever felt it before. Fraser was striding up and down clapping his hands and stamping his feet. He caught sight of me and bellowed, 'You should be acclimatising yourself, Connybear. This is just a taste.'

I swore, scuttled back into the compartment and took another swallow of Ollie Fisher's rum. We seemed to be at the top of a white and grey world. Looking out the window I could see the snow on the far peaks and the tops of dark pine trees closer around that looked to be inviting the snow to fall on them. A passenger had walked a short distance away from the train and had come hurrying back. Steam from his breath enveloped him. Charley looked out the window and chuckled.

'He don't know how soft this is. Shoulda done it by foot in '96, eh, Ollie?'

'Right. Carrying a hundred and fifty pound pack.'

'No pack animals?'

Ollie rubbed his lower jaw; the old skin stretched and was slow getting back into shape. The skin on his hands was cracked and parched. 'Bad winter,' he said. 'I ate my mule before I got to the top of the pass.'

'Me too. 'Course, we come at the right time – before the real rush,' Charley said. 'Next year those poor devils comin' up here died like rats. They killed each other, some of 'em. And they turned the trail into a lot of mud slides and . . . what d'you call them ice sheets, Ollie?'

'Glaciers,' Ollie said. 'Nothing to the country around the Mackenzie, of course.'

Charley dug him in the ribs. 'Shut up, sourdough, can't you see Hank here ain't feelin' too good?'

Charley was right; what with the hangover and that view of the frozen peaks from the top of the pass and the talk of eating mules I was feeling very queasy. I tried to remember what they'd served us up at school about the North Pole. All I could remember was some stuff about Captain Oates going outside and not coming back and Captain Scott eating the harness from the dog sleds.[11]

The train was rattling downgrade on the Canadian side, rushing around bends and almost scraping the walls of the rocky cuttings. Suddenly I heard a rumbling roar and then a screech of metal on metal and then there was pandemonium. The train was rocking as it rounded a bend and half the mountain seemed to be falling down ahead of us. Boulders came crashing down the slopes and trees were toppling end over end with their thick ends splayed like chewed matches.

'Slide!' Charley yelled. 'Jesus, there's a long way to fall.'

I looked over to the other side of the train; it was slowing down and the trees weren't whizzing by the windows as fast as they had been. If the rockslide hit the train it looked like it would sweep it off the tracks and over the side down a long slope. Not too steep but not regular either; surviving that drop would be a matter of luck. I couldn't help it, I felt I was all out of luck and couldn't take any chances on rocks and trees behaving the way they should. I grabbed my bag and headed for the rear door.

People were lurching around between the seats, grabbing bags and coats, standing and sitting and cursing like sailors. I pushed my way to the rear of the car, through the open door and jumped into the brush and loose rocks and dirt on the side away from the rockslide. As I took off I heard an almighty crash and felt the train shake under me. I closed my eyes and tried to curl into a ball, ready to roll.

I hit hard, got a face full of dirt and stones and jarred my legs and then my shoulder in the roll. But I was alive and I still had hold of my bag. I came to rest against a tree. That is, my head rapped sharply against it and my vision wobbled as I wrapped my free arm around it. I lay there gasping; I was just inches from a nasty drop and the grey clouds were wheeling around above me in a pale sky. I closed my eyes and fought for breath and a slower heart beat. When they came I looked up at the train. It had stopped before the rockslide and that cataclysm itself had subsided to a trickle of small rocks, slipping dirt and a cloud of dust. A big tree which must have been thrown sideways in the slide had hit the last carriage and knocked it half off the tracks. People were getting down gingerly on to the line at the rear and the engineer was up front inspecting the blockage. There was a shout and a knot of people rushed to the side of the tracks where a man was staggering and bleeding. He fell to his knees.

'Thrown clear off!' I heard someone yell and it was music to my ears. If people were being thrown clear off why couldn't Hank Connybear be one of them and be thrown clear back to the US border? I wriggled around behind the tree, taking care not to move closer to the edge and slowly wiped my face clear of dust and grit. I had some tears in my clothes but nothing serious; I was wearing heavy gloves so I hadn't lost any skin on my hands. All in all I was in good shape. A bottle would've been a help but I consoled myself with the thought that it probably wouldn't have survived the jump.

I stood up carefully and got a grip on my bag. My head was ringing but I could see clearly again. A little way along was a short drop to a ledge that ran parallel to the track but well below it and falling gradually down into the valley.

'Things could be worse, Dick,' I said. I bent low and started for the ledge.

'Could they indeed, Mr Connybear? I'll thank you to stand where you are.'

Sergeant Fraser stepped from behind a tree a few feet away. From my crouch he seemed to be at least eight feel tall and the long-barrel pistol he held in his hand looked like a howitzer.

CHAPTER EIGHT

They levered the carriage back on to the tracks and the engineer and some of the workman types on board the train had the line cleared pretty quickly. Most of the bigger boulders had gone on rolling down the valley and the smaller ones were easy to lever out of the way if you knew how. Charley Moon was one of those who helped, more in a supervisory category than with actual muscle, but I had no doubt he would have been useful in that department too.

Fraser had me virtually under guard. He sat beside me with his pistol in his coat pocket and he stood outside the convenience which I had to use pretty frequently. I was scared of what lay ahead. To arrive as a disgraced man in some godforsaken outpost, charged with the duty of self-rehabilitation, is one thing. Hard enough, but made a damn sight harder by bearing the reputation of a coward. That was the upshot of my jump from the train. All the other men aboard treated me with contempt, including Charley and Ollie, and the women turned their faces away when I looked at them.

I tried to explain to one of the school teachers that I'd been planning to lighten the load and be first on hand for the track-clearing but he didn't buy it.

'You pushed past women and children to jump, sir,' he said. 'It's a pity you didn't break your cowardly neck.'

Well, I hadn't noticed any children but I supposed I would have pushed past them regardless. So would you if you were being taken somewhere by a six and a half foot martinet to be despatched to the North Pole. Nowadays I'd just have to mention the Gulag and that Pasternak fellow and everyone would be on my side but then, with the worms eating the millions of slaughtered men in their graves, you had to be a man, a hero . . . bloody awful film, bloody Gyppo . . . [Browning breaks off here and rambles incoherently, evidently under the influence of alcohol. He appears to have confused the Russian Nobel Prizewinning writers Pasternak and Solzhenitsyn. The film he refers to above is probably 'Doctor Zhivago' in which Egyptian actor Omar Sharif had the leading role. The tape runs silently for a time and when Browning returns to his work his speech is interrupted by loud slurping, probably of coffee. His voice becomes steadier as he proceeds. Ed.]

We rattled down into the valley and to the end of the line — the town of Whitehorse. It was one of those places that seemed to be crowding towards the water. Parts of Sydney are like that, and San Francisco. You get the feeling that if they could have built the town out over the actual water they would have. The life of the town, such as it was, all took place along the street that fronted the Yukon River. I remember the river more than the town which isn't surprising as I was to spend more time on rivers than in towns over the weeks ahead.

Whitehorse was an unremarkable place — basically built of timber, like Skagway, and weathered to a dull grey where the paint hadn't been freshened up regularly. There were stores and saloons and banks (not built of timber), as well as the usual motley collection of official buildings — post office, city hall and fire station. The rest of the town away from the river was laid out in the boring grid that all gold towns seem to fall into once the roaring days are over. The barracks were large to house the sizable detachment of Mounted Police.

To my great relief, Fraser didn't think it necessary to report to the Mountie HQ in Whitehorse. Two steam boats had held their departure to accommodate the travellers from the delayed train, so it was all rush, rush down to the landing and stamping of tickets and mind your toes as we boarded the boat for the five hundred mile voyage to Dawson City.

The river, now that *was* remarkable. It was a peculiar green colour out in the middle away from the muddy banks and the places where canneries and other factories spilled their muck into it. Blue water under a blue sky I understand, and grey under grey, but the green water under the pale Yukon clouds with the rocky landscape was mysterious. Of course it wasn't all green; there was plenty of white water where the river broke up into rapids. The sight of that water rushing upon rocks was enough to chill your blood, if it wasn't already chilled by the wind. People told me later that in the rush of '98 the gold seekers took to the river in canoes and on rafts and whatever else they could rig up. No amount of gold could have got me to try it; we had an experienced river pilot who took us through the channels and treacherous currents as if he was just walking down the street avoiding the dog shit.

Four bargeloads of stores for Dawson went with us, one pulled by each boat and one pushed along in front – no problem, apparently, to the pilot. The accommodation was rough, bunks below decks for the lucky ones like Fraser and myself, shake-downs in the saloon and smoking rooms for the rest. A few Indians, half-breeds, trappers and other roughnecks had deck passages but I prefer not to think about that method of travel, especially at night.

Charley and Ollie were on the other boat but they might as well have been on the moon. I was in Coventry. The story of my jump from the train had spread among the boat passengers and they seemed to have got wind of my standing as a Mountie as well. Fraser watched me closely for the first few hours after we'd stowed our bags, but he could see that I was in a sort of prison of my own making and he took himself off to yarn with the other amateur ornithologists and ethnologists aboard.

That first day on the river was one of the most miserable I can recall. No one spoke to me other than to ask me to get out of the way or to ask if I wanted tea or coffee with my food. There were card and dice games going on and money changing hands, but I would have been as welcome as a bad smell. I rolled into my bunk early and spent a fitful night under thin blankets and with cold feet despite three pairs of socks.

The next day I discovered a small commissary on the boat, open for a few hours only. I bought tobacco and whisky, what else? The storekeeper was a fat, grizzled individual who doubled as a cook on the boat. Stuck in the kitchen and the store, he seemed to be the only person on the boat who didn't know of my shameful past. After I'd stated my wants he put on a pair of half-moon glasses and peered at me. I stared back, ready for a fight. His face was incredibly puckered and lined, making his age impossible to guess.

'You a breed?' he asked.

'No.'

'French?'

'No. Why the hell would it matter?'

He put the whisky on the counter and reached under it for tobacco. 'Don't have to sell firewater to breeds and I don't like to sell it to French.'

'What's wrong with the French?'

'They stink. You want soap?'

My patience left me. I grabbed the front of his greasy coat and pulled him towards me. He was small, not more than five foot four, and I was able to get good leverage on him. 'Is that why you asked me if I was French? Are you saying I stink? Eh?' I turned my fist and bunched the front of his shirt up around his neck. Suddenly I felt a sharp dig in my crotch.

'You do stink, mister,' he said. 'An' if you don't let me go I'll blow your balls off with this gut shooter. Let go!'

He had a derringer jammed between my legs. He dug the business end in savagely and I released him.

'Shit,' I said. 'I should've known I couldn't take a trick. Just give me the grog and the tobacco and tell me what I owe you.'

'You sound depressed, friend.' He straightened his clothes and slammed a cake of yellow soap down on the counter beside the sack of Bull Durham. 'Five dollars for the whisky, fifty cents for the tobacco, five cents for the soap.'

I counted out the money. 'You keep it in round figures.'

'Yup. Five cents for papers – packet of five.'

'Matches?'

'Ten cents – packet of ten.'

'You should be a pimp. You could have a twenty dollar whore, a ten dollar and a five dollar.'

'Not a bad idea. You want a drink?'

'Sure.'

He unscrewed the cap on my bottle and produced two shot glasses which he filled to the brim. He tossed his back, filled it again and raised it slowly.

'Good luck to you, whoever you are an' whatever you're doin'.'

I drank. 'I'm a Mountie,' I said bitterly. 'And I'm being posted to the Mackenzie River, so I'm going to need the luck.'

'You sure are. Well, you don't look like no Mountie.'

'More like a breed or a Frenchman?'

'Right. There's some Mounties with beards in Dawson but they don't look like you.' He ran his pink, scrubbed hand across his fat, stubbled cheeks. 'More clipped, you know? An' more just with moustaches. An' that hair! Ain't nobody goin' to believe you're a Mountie with that hair.'

I nodded, finished my drink and collected my purchases.

'One for the road?' he said.

I put the bottle in my pocket. 'Sure. One for the river, let's say. Where's *your* bottle, friend?'

He grinned and reached for the shutter to pull down over the counter. 'Store's closed,' he said.

I went to a sheltered part of the deck and took a few nips on the bottle and rolled myself a couple of cigarettes. After another hefty slug and with a fat cigarette well alight, I felt well enough to take up a position by the rail and take in the view. I'd travelled the Hawkesbury River by boat many times; in some ways the scenery wasn't so different – low scrub and rocky banks – but the temperature was about fifty degrees lower and that icy green water was nothing like the soft blue of the Hawkesbury which you can swim in for nine months of the year if you don't mind the sharks.

I was feeling warmed by the whisky and tobacco, but homesick and very sorry for myself, when a long, thin shadow blotted out the pale sunshine.

'Ah, Connybear,' Fraser said. 'I've been looking for you.'

'You've found me, Sergeant.'

'Not thinking of bolting again, are you?' As I've said, I only once heard a humorous remark from Fraser. He wasn't joking now. We were passing through a deep gorge; the river had narrowed and there were nasty-looking prongs of rocks sticking out into the water. The walls of the gorge were steep, sheer in places. Maybe Doug Fairbanks could have climbed them with a bit of rope and a grappling iron or two but even that was doubtful.

'No, Sergeant,' I said glumly. 'I'm resigned to my fate.'

'That's not the spirit, not the spirit at all. I'm sure there's better stuff than that in you, Connybear. Come with me, there's somebody aboard I want you to meet.'

I followed him to the smoking room where a young man, brown haired and bearded, was squatting in a corner sorting through a collection of arctic gear – snow-shoes, goggles, anti-magnetic compasses.

'Fitzgerald,' Fraser said, 'I want you to meet Henry Connybear. Connybear's a constable in the Force and an old Yukon hand.'

Fitzgerald stood. He was only an inch or two shorter than Fraser but he was much wider and thicker through. He was holding a fur mitten in his hand and the thought came to me that if he was wearing furs he'd resemble a grizzly bear. His handshake was strong enough to cut off the circulation at the shoulder.

'Pleased to meet you,' he said.

I grunted, thinking of the bottle in my coat and feeling the need for another cigarette.

'Fitzgerald here has a most interesting project in hand,' Fraser said.

'Oh, really?' I was irritated already by Fitzgerald's upright stance and steady gaze. 'Is he going to spend the winter with the Indians or something?'

'That *is* an adventure,' Fraser said. 'Done it myself more than once. But no, this is to do with the traditions of the Force.'

I looked more closely at Fitzgerald. There was something vaguely familiar about him but I couldn't place it. The name meant something too. But I wasn't really interested enough to search my memory. 'The traditions of the Force, eh?' I said. 'That's probably more in your line than mine, Sergeant. Nice to have met you, Fitzgerald. I think I'll just . . .'

'Hold hard, Connybear. This is important; surely you've heard of the Dawson Patrol?'

'Er, yes, well . . .' I dimly remembered reading something about it in Burton Deane – a five-man patrol setting out from somewhere and not making it to somewhere else. Reminded me of Burke and Wills[12]. What was the name of the mad bastard in charge? . . . One of those hero-of-the-empire types . . . Fitzsimmons? No, Fitzgerald, that was it, Fitzgerald!

A gleam came into young Fitzgerald's eye and he seemed to pull himself up even straighter. 'It was 1908,' he said. 'One of the worst winters on record. My uncle attempted to travel from the Mackenzie River to Dawson in twenty days. It had never been done. They said it couldn't be done.'

'They were right as I recall,' I said. 'Didn't all five of them starve to death?'

'One took his own life,' Fraser said. 'Took the coward's way out.'

'That's debatable,' I said. 'Well, Fitzgerald, you've come to do a bit of sightseeing, have you? See where a bit of family history took place? Good luck to you.'

'That's not it,' Fitzgerald said. 'I'm going to lead a party from Dawson to the Mackenzie and back inside forty days. I'm not going to use any of the food caches or markers they've put in since my uncle's day. I'm going to show that he was right, that it was possible, with the right men. With men like him!'

I've met plenty of them since – clear eyes, square jaws and concrete for brains. Thinking back, young Fitzgerald reminds me of Gene Tunney[13] with a dash of Charles Lindbergh thrown in. Dangerous men to be around. I reached for my tobacco sack and felt the comfort of the bottle. 'Best of luck. Bit close down here, I . . .'

Fraser barred my way. 'I want you and Edward to have a long talk, Connybear.'

'Why?'

'He's going to be recruiting a party from among the men of the Force at Dawson. Your Yukon experience will be invaluable and, not to mince matters, you need a chance to rehabilitate yourself. I'm going to make a strong recommendation, and I think it'll carry some weight, that you be a member of Fitzgerald's party.'

CHAPTER NINE

Dawson City was bigger than I expected. It sprawled out in all directions around the centre which featured some solid two and three storey buildings as well as the lower, meaner kind. The place was at the meeting point of the Yukon and Klondike rivers and those two words dominated it. If a tavern wasn't 'The Yukon' it was 'The Klondike' and if a thoroughfare wasn't Klondike Street it was Yukon Road.

I picked up these impressions as I walked through the streets with Fraser to the Mounted Police Headquarters. The sky was a clear, pale blue and the light wind had an edge that was just a little blunter than a razor. Everybody I saw was puffing on a pipe or a cigar or cigarette and I decided that the air was too cold to breath comfortably into the lungs. You can see that I was in a thoughtful frame of mind and I had two things in particular to think about.

Back on the boat, a few hours out of Dawson, Fraser had come upon me standing in front of a mirror with a pair of scissors in my hand and a razor and shaving brush at the ready. I was about to hack into my hair which was then on my shoulders when he stayed my hand.

'What d'you think you're doing, Connybear?'

'Getting shipshape, sir,' I said. 'Smartening up. Don't want to let the Force down by a sloppy appearance, do I?'

'I take that to be a joke,' Fraser said. He tipped out my hot water and closed the razor. 'Sometimes I think you haven't got the sense of a papoose. Where you're going a man needs all the protection he can get. Leave your hair and beard the way they are. Your superiors will make allowances. Save your dandying up for when you get back to Dawson from the Mackenzie in under forty days.'

That was all right with me. It sounded like I could have some privileges and be a bit of a hero in advance of the actual heroism which is always the best way around, especially as I had no intention of going any closer to the Arctic Circle than I was already.

Still, it was a pretty villainous face that looked at me from the mirror. My skin, that part of it not covered by hair, had taken on a yellowish tinge and my eyes had developed a sort of slanty, tight-lidded look in the cold; my hair was long as I've said and a punch I'd taken back in the brawl with Reuben Dawes seemed to have flattened the end of my nose somewhat. Strong white teeth were about my only good feature.

The second curious happening had been Charley Moon's wave from the ship. Fraser and I, being younger and less burdened with baggage than Charley and Ollie, had got away first. By chance I looked back at the steamer from the dock and I saw Charley Moon standing by the rail. He saw me too and he took off his bowler hat and waved it wildly, as friendly and enthusiastic as could be, just as he'd been on our boozy night in Skagway, and as if my disgraceful jump from the train hadn't happened. Puzzling.

As we tramped the boards in front of the shops and negotiated the muddy cross streets, Fraser's usual dour demeanour seemed to give way to actual bad temper. He kicked at a dog that scuttled across in front of him and I thought I heard him swear under his breath. Fraser discomforted was something worth pursuing.

'Tell me, Sergeant, what is it that brings you to Dawson? You seemed to enjoy the trip up well enough, but you don't seem too happy now you're here.'

'Damn foolishness,' Fraser growled.

'What is?'

'Perhaps you're not a complete fool after all, Connybear. You're right, I came for the travel. I love that inner passage and those Alaskan Mountains. You'll laugh, but I feel close to God when I see them.'

I knew better than to laugh, though I had to stop to light a cigarette to get through the moment. 'But now you're here . . .'

'I'm here to advise on celebrations for next year. It's the fiftieth year since the Force was formed. Celebrations! What do I know of such things? I'd celebrate by crossing Canada from west to east. I have to say I envy you, Connybear. You'll be doing a man's job, not sitting about with cups of tea nattering to pen-pushers and their wives.'

'I'd change places with you, Sergeant,' I said. 'Any day, just say the word.'

Life in the Mounties was as close to life in the army as makes no difference. If you've not endured it you're lucky and it can be summed up as a mixture of hard work and boredom, hard beds and bad food. Things went off more or less as Fraser had said they would. I was given a rude rebuke by the commanding officer for my neglect of duty in Vancouver and I got the cold shoulder from almost everyone on account of the story having got around of my jump from the train. Give him his due though, Fraser put me forward for the Dawson Patrol idea with vigour and enthusiasm and managed to convey the impression that I was keen to go. I played up to this and after a week or so I was the forthcoming hero of the frozen north rather than the despised scallywag[14] of the south.

Fitzgerald had got official approval for his mad scheme and I spent some time in training for the escapade. We harnessed up dog sleds, loaded them with wood and pushed them through the grass because there wasn't yet enough snow to practise on. It was exhausting and tedious and bloody cold, even without the snow. At first I thought it would be easier than the regular Mountie drill

– up at dawn, parading, maintaining equipment and so forth, but after a while I began to wonder. After the first solid snowfall, when Fitzgerald pushed us over ten miles of the stuff in one day – uphill both ways or so it seemed – I was in no doubt. I'd rather do the midnight to 4 a.m. guard watch – the coldest and most boring job in the Force – for a year on end than take a step towards the Mackenzie River with that whooping, hollering, 'Mush'-yelling madman.

Apart from me and Fitzgerald there were two others whose names I forget. One was a retired Mountie[15] who was to act as guide and the other was something of a greenhorn. He was younger than the rest of us, including Fitzgerald, and immensely strong. The joke among us was that he could pull a sled himself if need be. Privately, I wondered if he could do it with me riding on his shoulders because I was damn sure that I wouldn't survive five miles of the real thing.

The great thing in life, I've found, is to know what you want. If you're unsure about that you can't possibly act in your own best interest. (Perhaps what I *really* mean is that the great thing in life is to be able always to act in your own best interest.) Anyway, I knew what I wanted and that was to be well away in the other direction before the Fitzgerald party set out. Having spent some time in the army I knew the first rule of duty avoidance – malinger. After one of the snow runs I contrived to catch my foot in a sled, fall heavily and twist an ankle.

'How is it, Hank?' Fitzgerald said as he bent over me and exhaled frosty breath on my face.

'Think the damn thing's sprained,' I groaned.

'Good practice. Get up on it and let's complete the run. We could all get sprained ankles, torn thigh muscles and the like. Let's see how they affect us.'

He was serious. I staggered up; the ankle did hurt although not very much. I stumbled, groaned and collapsed over the sled.

'Think he's fainted, Cap,' the young Atlas said. 'You want me to carry him or put him on the sled? It ain't but five miles.'

'I want him to walk!' Fitzgerald snorted.

I lay as still as a stone – damn uncomfortable it was too, lying across that stacked wood.

'Don't reckon he will,' said the guide. 'We gotta keep movin', Mr Fitzgerald. Do us no good at all to stand around here in the cold. We'll stiffen up.'

'Sling him over the sled, then.' I opened one eye and saw Fitzgerald march off to the front. Atlas rearranged me on the sled and I spent the rest of the journey groaning and thrashing around. I hoped they'd take it for pain – in reality, I was trying to get more comfortable.

So I did my second stint in the infirmary, all within a few months of 'joining' the Mounties. That's probably a record. This infirmary was much the same as the one in Vancouver except that there was no wise-ass orderly like Dagberry around (and no recreation like 'Klondike' Angie, more's the pity). As it turned out, my ankle was pretty badly twisted. The doctor, a red-faced old fool with food-stained whiskers, assured me that the ankle would be as good as new by the time of the patrol and no amount of complaint I set up, or hobbling I did, could convince him otherwise.

Fitzgerald was anxious about my progress and received the doctor's optimistic reports gladly. You may wonder at this. After all, I'd hardly been a tower of strength on the training marches and I hadn't shown any particular woodcraft or skill at direction-finding in the snow to justify my reputation as an old Yukon hand. But Fitzgerald wanted me along because I'd made two mistakes. The first was that I'd shown him I was an excellent shot. Shooting in the snow is bloody hard: the light is tricky, the gloves and clothes are an encumbrance and range is hard to judge. I'd knocked over a running hare with a rifle, shooting uphill at some impossible range and Fitzgerald had cheered me to the echo.

'Bravo, Connybear!' He'd raced up and clapped me on the back. 'We'll be travelling very light, dangerously light some might say.

Food weighs heavy. With you along, shooting like that, we can count on some game. I'd say I can trim off another twenty pounds.'

This hadn't made me popular with the other members of the party, but there you are. You can't please everyone. The second mistake was in revealing my fondness for, and abilities with, dogs. I couldn't help it, I've always had a way with dogs; the huskies were splendid animals and they took to me as much as I took to them. The husky is part wolf and part whatever other hardy breed happens to be part of its ancestry. They are strong dogs, but not very big or heavy. I found them intelligent and affectionate and had less trouble rounding them up and getting them harnessed and willing to work than the other members of the party. Men like Fitzgerald don't evaluate people the way you or I might – is he good chap? – does he like a drink and a joke? They weigh their usefulness, and first class shot and dog-handler *extraordinaire* Henry Connybear was acceptable material for our intrepid leader whatever his other shortcomings might be.

So my ankle wasn't going to save me. I was out of bed in a few days and the doctor promised me I'd be knee deep in snow again within a fortnight. I thanked him and contemplated shooting off a toe. Meanwhile, I was assigned light clerical duties in the office of the Commissioner for the Mounted Police in the Yukon Territory. I was put under the command of a sergeant who seemed to have very little to do. What duties he did have he quickly off-loaded on to me and absented himself. What he found to do in Dawson by day I can't imagine for it was a very dull, business-like place which only livened up on Friday and Saturday nights. I shuffled paper, signed for in-coming things and addressed out-going things and was generally bored stiff. One day, for want of anything better to do, and in hope of finding some loose cash or a forgotten bottle, I decided to clean up the office.

I swept and tidied and went through the drawers in the old rolltop desk throwing away more than I saved. I was about to toss out a bundle of dusty papers tied with a frayed blue ribbon when something under a folded back corner caught my eye. It was a part of a profile photograph, just the top half of the head but it said something to me. I untied the ribbon; the papers were old 'Wanted' posters dating back twenty years and more. I blew the dust off and spread out the paper which had attracted my attention. 'Wanted', it read along the top in bold letters, 'for Robbery & Murder.' Under the legend were two profile photographs; a large full face picture dominated the centre of the paper. The man depicted had a round face with cropped hair. It was evidently a photograph of a prisoner for he wore no hat and had a rough-looking denim shirt; the place where the number would have been had been blanked out.

The wanted man was Matthew Tolliver, alias Matt Oliver and several other variants on the name. He was described as five feet eight inches tall, 160 pounds and of a ruddy complexion. A former associate of the notorious Soapy Smith, Tolliver was wanted for the murder of a Mounted Policeman and the wounding of several citizens in Whitehorse in 1897, when he and two other gunmen robbed the Yukon Bank of one hundred and ninety thousand dollars. One thousand dollars was offered as a reward for the taking of Tolliver dead or alive.

Under this document was another in similar terms relating to Robert Carter, also known as Coldknife. Carter was described as a half-breed Han Indian – the picture was a drawing showing a glowering individual with black hair, slanted eyes and a wispy dark moustache. Making allowances for years, weight and grey hair, Matthew Tolliver and Coldknife were the men I knew as Ollie Fisher and Charley Moon.

CHAPTER TEN

I pocketed the posters and went about the rest of my duties in something of a daze for the rest of the day. This had to be useful information. Fisher and Moon had money and I had none, or very little. That was a fact. Charley had said he would help me if I wanted to get away. Also a fact. He'd given me the cold shoulder from the time I'd jumped train until Dawson, but then there was that puzzling wave from the boat. One thing was sure, Fisher and Moon must have known a way to escape from the Yukon Territory because they'd got away scot free with a fortune twenty-five years before. I tried to tell myself that twenty-five years wasn't such a long time; once a good man always a good man, and things like that, but I wasn't sure.

I also wasn't sure whether a 'Wanted' poster issued a quarter of a century back was still valid. And, for that matter, whether the rewards were still on offer. I had a lot to think about as I ate the inevitable evening meal of tough steak, watery potatoes and tasteless beans in the mess. In defiance of all regulations I had a bottle of brandy back in the hut I shared with three other constables. I chewed and swallowed fast, thinking that with luck they might linger over the coffee and give me time for a few stimulating snorts while I pondered my situation.

I ignored all greetings, raised at least three pairs of eyebrows when I refused a game of cards, and was on my way to my quarters when one of the daily orderlies approached me.

'Letter for you, Connybear,' he said. He held out a violet-tinted envelope and smirked.

'Don't wait around for your tip,' I snarled. I stuffed the letter into my pocket and headed for the brandy.

There was nothing fancy about my quarters – a large room with too-thin walls, small windows and a few tatty skins on the floor. There was a big wood stove without which life would have been impossible. We got a taste of that impossibility a few times when the man whose turn it was neglected to replenish the wood supply. I was guilty of it myself once and the offence caused sharp words and punches to be thrown. There was plenty of wood, however, on this occasion and I stoked the stove, poured some brandy into a mug and sat down to contemplate my options.

With a fair bit of brandy consumed and several cigarettes smoked, there was a nice, warm fug built up inside me and the room, but I was still no clearer on what to do. I stretched forward to put more wood on and heard the crinkle of the letter in my pocket. I had quite forgotten it. I poured another slug and opened the envelope. I have the letter beside me now as I record this. The writing is faint but I can still read it because she had a big, clear, round, childish hand.

Royalton Hotel,
Seattle, USA.

Dear Hank,

Ever since our wonderful time together I have been thinking about what you said about conning up to see you in the Yukon territory. I never had such a good time with any man before and I miss it I mean you most terrible.

But Hank – I know you are not Hank really but somebody else I don't know who. But I am sure we could be happy together whoever you are. I decided to go to Vancouver again and talk to the man in the hospital Constable Dagberry about you. He told me who he thinks you are and what you done and the terrible trouble you might be in.

But Hank – I don't care. I've got some money not much but enough to get a start maybe in a saloon or like that. I'm coming up to see you around Christmas time object matrimony as they say. I'm sure we could be happy and your secret will always be safe with me.

All my love,

This horrible thing is signed 'Angela'. [Regrettably, the letter from Angela has not so far been found among Browning's effects. Prior to his death at the avocado ranch in 1984, Browning's papers, clothes and other possessions seem to have been considerably disturbed, probably by creditors in the main but also by women with whom he was involved. The letter may have been a casualty of this disturbance. Ed.]

I heard footsteps outside the door and had to shove the letter quickly away. I was lighting a cigarette when one of my hutmates came in. He looked suspiciously at me as I licked the last drops out of my mug, but the bottle was safely away and no man in the Force would think of going through another man's traps. That made the Mounties unlike the army, where pilfering was the normal thing. In the Mounties it would have been regarded as the next worst thing to being a fairy. My hutmate strode across the room and warmed himself at the stove.

'Good fire, Connybear,' he said.

'Yes,' says I.

'Fancy a game of checkers?' He got out the board and set it up without waiting for me to answer. It saved having to talk to him – he never talked when he played checkers as the game took all his concentration – and there was nothing else to do anyway. You see what I mean about boredom being a big part of life in the Royal Canadian Mounted Police?

I didn't get a lot of sleep that night even though I sneaked a few sly snorts of brandy under the bedclothes. I felt myself to be surrounded by red-coated enemies determined to send me to an icy death in the company of a mad nephew of a mad uncle. I'd read up a bit on the original Dawson Patrol and what I learned appalled me. Fitzgerald the Elder must have been one of the stubbornest, most blind-to-reason Irishmen in history, and there have been a lot to choose from. Something about the look in the nephew's eye suggested to me that he was of the same ilk. If he couldn't prove the Fitzgeralds to have been right and cover himself in glory, burial forever in some snowdrift on the trail would be his second preference.

The imminent arrival of Angie, hellbent on blackmailing me into marriage, was the last straw. I took the drinks under the blankets partly to warm myself, partly to help me sleep and partly to get my courage up. I was in a spot but I had a weapon – the information I possessed about Ollie Fisher and Charley Moon also known as Matthew Tolliver and Coldknife. The question was – would I have the guts to use it?

On the following Friday at 9 p.m. I was off-duty and wearing a pea jacket over dungarees with heavy boots. I had a woollen cap on my head and my service pistol was in the pocket of the jacket. I also had a month's pay with me as well as the 'Wanted' posters on Ollie and Charley. I was scheduled to begin work in the snow with Fitzgerald again the following week. My ankle had mended sufficiently and I was several days closer to the arrival of 'Klondike' Angie. I was as ready as I'd ever be.

The obvious place to look for Ollie and Charley was a saloon but, as there were several of those in Dawson, as well as restaurants and at least a couple of whorehouses which, as I came to think about it, were also logical places, the job might not be too easy. I must have had an instinct for this kind of work – which I put to good use in Los Angeles a lot later when I was a licensed private eye – I mean finding people. It's partly laziness; I had no partiality to tramping all over town on a cold night poking my nose into whisky dens and houses of ill fame, but it's also good sense. If you want to reach someone, discover where they sleep and you've just about done the job. I've found it holds true whether the place is the Beverly Hilton or a *barrio* flophouse. And the best method to locate the domicile is to use the telephone.

I installed myself with a pot of coffee and a flask of brandy in a cafe on the west edge of town. Finding a congenial place with a telephone hadn't been easy and had involved a bit of scouting around. As I set about calling the first hotel I reflected that this wasn't such a bad thing. When dealing with desperadoes like Ollie and Charley, even if they were somewhat rusty ones, it was best to know the lie of the land.

'This is Sergeant Connybear of the Mounted Police. I'm trying to locate two friends of mine – Messrs Oliver Fisher and Charles Moon. Would they happen to be staying in your establishment?'

'No, Sergeant.'

This was the response I got for almost an hour. The coffee was finished and so was the brandy and I began to draw dark looks from the proprietor for hogging the telephone even though I was paying extra for the calls. My throat was raw from smoking as I croaked the question to the desk clerk at the Commercial Hotel.

'Yes, Sergeant,' came the reply. 'Mr Fisher and Mr Moon have the Lucky Strike suite.'

'Is that a fact? That's just fine. Are they in at present?'

'Why no, sir. They went out on the town with two . . . young women. They're real characters, those two.'

'That's right, they are. Would it be all right if I came over to wait for them?'

'You could wait in the lobby, Sergeant, is it? I'm afraid I couldn't let you up to the suite unless you're on official . . .'

'No. No. The lobby would be fine. Have you got a good fire?'

'Certainly.'

'Can I get a drink?'

'Yes. I could arrange some company for you if . . .'

'No. That'll be all right. I'll be along directly.'

Well, I should've just thought it through a bit more. All I needed to do was ask which hotel in town laid on the best whores for the guests and I could have saved myself a lot of trouble and expense. I paid for the last call, pulled my coat collar up and walked out into the street. A light snow had fallen while I was in the cafe. The moon was up and I could see the snow on the high ground around the town and watch it collecting in hollows and other sheltered spots as I walked. There were a few cars and horse-drawn vehicles in the streets and some people hurrying along trying to prevent the snow from collecting on their hats and running down their necks. The roads started to turn white and the wheels made thin, dark tracks across them. A light wind got up and blew the snowflakes into my eyes. I felt a long, long way from Sydney where, so far as I know, it has not snowed since the dawn of time.[16]

The Commercial Hotel was at the other end of town, a stone's throw from the river and with high pine trees on all sides. I stomped along the path up to the glassed-in porch where in the summertime I guess the folks could sit and look at the river and the hills and think about taking off their sweaters. Right now snow was accumulating on the ledges and I had to kick some back before I could open the door. I went through to the lobby where a couple of decent-sized logs were blazing and up to the desk where the clerk was rubbing his hands. He was a small man with a slicked-down cowlick and sharp blue eyes. Behind the desk looked like the coldest place in the room.

'Yessir?' he said.

'Connybear. I telephoned a while back.'

'You've tracked snow into the lobby.'

'Sorry. I won't be the last. You said I could wait for Ollie and Charley.'

'Well . . .' He looked at me dubiously. Perhaps he thought I'd arrive in scarlet coat and riding breeches and throw him a salute. I was annoyed but I as sure as hell didn't want to go out in the cold again. I produced a silver dollar and laid it on the desk.

'What's your name, mister?'

'Claude Calwell, sir.'

'Well, Claude. Why don't you go along to the bar and get me a whisky and a cigar and a drink for yourself if you've a mind and put the change in your pocket and forget about the snow?'

He took the coin in a red, chafed hand. 'I'm not allowed to drink on duty, but I'll be happy to oblige you, . . . Sergeant.' I installed myself by the fire, opened my coat and let some of the warmth in. Claude brought the drink and lit my cigar for me. I puffed smoke, sipped whisky and maybe I nodded off for a while because it seemed like no time at all before I heard the door to the porch slam and a mixture of high female and low male laughter, drunk in both cases.

'Well, look who it ain't!' Ollie practically twisted the blonde woman's head off getting her to lift it and look at me, "s our ol' pal, Frank . . .'

'Hank,' Charley Moon said. He was following the other two. He had no companion and seemed steadier which still put him a long way on the other side of sober. 'Howdy, Hank. Heard you was off to the North Pole mighty soon.'

I stood and faced them. I could feel the pistol in one pocket and what might be their death warrants in another. I didn't feel comfortable though, especially as Charley seemed to get more sober by the second and looked ready to throw a chair, shoot out the lights or do whatever was necessary.

The croak had come back into my voice. 'Like to talk with you, Charley.'

'Be my pleasure. Here or in our suit?'

'That's suite, silly,' the woman giggled.

'Wherever's private,' I said.

'Let's go up then,' Charley said. 'We can close a door or two an' open a bottle or three. Ollie'd probably like to be excused. That right, Ollie?'

For an answer Ollie slapped his blonde's broad, green satin-covered rump. We climbed the stairs in order of drunkenness, that is to say, Ollie first, then the blonde, then Charley and me in the rear. The Lucky Strike suite was a series of connected rooms – sitting rooms, bedrooms, bathrooms and the like. The central sitting room had a deep carpet and wallpaper depicting scenes from the Klondike goldfields. Ollie and the blonde went giggling and slapping off into one of the rooms and Charley watched them go. He shucked off his raincoat, threw it over a chair and bent down to a put a match to the wood and paper that was waiting in the big fireplace. When the blaze was to his satisfaction he moved into a chair and gestured for me to sit on the other side of the hearth.

'You look like a man with something on your mind, Hank,' he said. 'And seeing how my girl didn't last the distance I've got nothing to do but listen.' He laughed and pulled a cigar from his jacket pocket. 'And I don't much fancy listenin' to that old goat tryin' to get it up. So, what's on your mind, Hank?'

'My name isn't Hank Connybear, it's Dick Browning. Just as yours isn't Charley Moon.' I took the posters out of my pocket and spread them on my knee. I also took out my pistol and pointed it at the third button of his swelling waistcoat. 'It's Robert Carter or, if you prefer, Coldknife.'

He looked at me for a minute, then he got his cigar lit. After the first puff he burst into a deep, gurgling laugh. Tobacco and whisky fumes rushed across the space towards me. 'Well, Hank . . .' scuse me . . . Dick or whatever the hell you want to call yourself. I'm powerful glad that you've made your move.'

'What d'you mean?' I held the pistol steady; that's one thing I can do no matter how scared I am.

'First time I saw you I thought you was just the man for an important job Ollie and me have in mind. But until right now I didn't know if you was ever goin' to be desperate an' mean enough. Well, you are. Put the gun away and let's have a drink.'

CHAPTER ELEVEN

Charley (I never got into the way of calling him Robert and Coldknife seemed a mite unfriendly), filled me in on the *true* story of how he and Ollie struck it rich in '97. There certainly wasn't much back-breaking labour to it. Along with another man named Daniels, they robbed the bank.

'And killed a Mountie,' I interjected at that point in the tale.

'Pity, that,' Charley said. 'T'weren't intentional. It was a stray bullet, might not even have been fired by us but that's the way they told it.'

'And they would've hung you for it.'

'Yup. Three on a meat hook if they coulda catched us.'

'How did you get away?'

'You're rushin' me. Want a drink?'

I considered it but I still wasn't comfortable with Charley. His jacket was big and loose enough to hold a small gun and from the way he moved, like when he bent to light the fire and straightened up, all very smooth, I didn't doubt that he could still move fast if he had to. 'No drink,' I said.

'Suit y'self. I see you've still got that six shooter in reach.'

'That's right.'

'You any good with it?'

'Good enough.'

'Might have to be. Well, to get on with the story, Matt . . . you know who I mean?'

'Call him what you like.'

'Yup. Matt and Fancy Daniels, that was what he was called on account of the duds he wore – coloured weskits and such – we rode outa town, it was about this time o' year, you understand, roads an' trails still open, an' we got up into the hills and started a landslide.' He grinned at the quarter-of-a-century-old memory. 'Blocked the roads an' we had the best mountain ponies in the Territory.'

'So you all got away and lived happily ever after.'

'Nope. First thing you have to understand was that a lot of the loot was in gold, dust an' nuggets, and gold is heavy.'

'So I've heard back home – Ballarat and places like that.'

Charley grinned. 'Knew you was an Aussie, somehow. Well, that's all to the good. As well as divvying up the loot we had to divide the gold an' paper money. Now, Matt and me was strong young fellows then an' we could carry just about anything. Not so with Daniels, though. He'd done spent his life in saloons an' brothels so he had lung disease and plenty of other things wrong with him. He could ride 'n' shoot all right, an' play cards an' drink an' poke girls, but he couldn't lift nor carry worth a damn.'

'But you had horses,' I said.

'Sure we did. We had horses all the way to where we took to the rivers.'

'Rivers?'

'Best way outa the Territory then an' now. Bein' an Indian, half leastways, I knew some people who could help us. We travelled by river an' creek way to the south an' then we had horses again. That is, Matt 'n' me did but poor ol' Fancy didn't. His horse fell and broke its leg. Fancy had to shoot it.'

'Where was this?'

'I'll get to that. This left Fancy with his paper money an' his gold an' no way to travel.'

'What about you and Ollie?'

'We was willin' to take Fancy up behind us in turns an' his paper money but not his gold. That'd be too much for the ponies.'

'So . . . ?'

'So Fancy had to bury his gold.'

'Ah, and you know where.'

'More or less.'

'Daniels didn't get back to it?'

'He was shot to death in Butte, Montana not long after we made it down to the United States. We split up as soon as we crossed over. Matt 'n' me travelled together a while but we went our separate ways too.'

'And prospered.'

Charley threw his cigar butt in the fire. 'Yeah, I guess. But there's not a man alive wouldn't want an extra hundred and fifty thousand dollars.'

'How much?'

'You heard. Not long back Ollie found out how soon after our great escape Fancy cashed in his chips. He asked around, talked gold to folks who knew, and he calculates that the gold Fancy Daniels buried is worth about that figure now. Untraceable, an' there for the takin'.'

'Where for the taking?'

'Ah, now that there's the point. Matt 'n' me's too old for the trip. What we come up here to do was to find someone to make the trip for us.'

'I see.'

'Figured you would. It'd be tough. There'd be walkin' or dog sled travel, plus some time in a canoe and then some time on horseback. You can ride, can't you?'

'Better than most.'

'Knew you was the man for the job.'

'You'd trust me with a hundred and fifty thousand dollars?'

'Nope. There's only one way across the border in the parts you'd be travellin' to. Matt 'n' me'd be there waitin'.'

'What would my share be?'

'One sixth. Twenty five thousand.'

'That's a hell of a lot to me but it doesn't seem like so much for you and Ollie . . . Matt.'

'No, well, it ain't really. But the truth is it gets kinda dull just sitting around old an' rich. I had a hankerin' to see my country again. Matt, well, he's willin' to go on the river himself if he has to. He wants one last adventure, it looks like. Mind you, it *would* be his last. I ain't so foolish.'

'What guarantee have I got that you wouldn't just shoot me after I bring out the gold?'

'None. But like you say, the actual money don't mean all that much to us. An' what choice have you got, Dick? It's my scheme or the Mackenzie for you. An' remember this – you'd be goin' south towards the land of the free an' the brave.'

'And the rich,' I said.

'That's what you'll be if'n it all works out.'

'What're the odds, Charley? And I will have a drink now if you've got one handy.'

'You're seein' the light, brother.' He walked in that slinky, light-footed way he had across the room and opened a cabinet. 'Rye or bourbon?'

'Either.'

With a glass in my hand and the rye warming my throat, the prospect didn't look so bleak. I listened as Charley outlined the plan; he would provide the initial transport and provisions and could arrange for me to meet an Indian who would travel with me to and down the river. He said he'd draw a map showing me where to leave the river and where to go on horseback, first to Fancy Daniels' cache and then to the border and freedom. It all sounded easy, poor fool that I was.

'Matt'll be disappointed,' Charley said.

'Why?' I held out my glass for a re-charge.

'He was hopin' to go himself, like I said. When you jumped offa the train he done give up on you.'

'But you didn't?'

'Nope. I figured you was a survivor an' that's what we want.'

'You're right. I'm a survivor.'

'Good. That's a quality goin' to be in demand.'

I thought back to those words of Charley Moon's many times in the weeks that followed. At first, everything went smoothly enough. Charley convinced his partner that I was the man for the job after all. Fitzgerald had outfitted his victims pretty thoroughly, so I was well kitted-up for the trip south. I was even able to get my hands on a Winchester '73 lever action rifle which was one of the few firearms the patrol was going to take. A shotgun would have been an asset but as Fitzgerald's sainted uncle hadn't taken one (and therefore probably helped to condemn his men to death by starvation because birds were the only game available), young Fitz wouldn't have one along.

It had come on to snow heavily and this decided the mode of transport for the first leg. Charley spent the Saturday acquiring a sled and provisions and most of Sunday morning packing and strapping the sled. I occupied myself with the dogs, getting to know them and letting them get used to me. I also met the Indian, a grim-faced, squat little fellow named Eli Hardpebble who spoke minimal English in such a guttural tone it was hard to understand him. I practised my few words of Kutchin which seemed to please him. That is, his face relaxed from its clenched, hatchet-in-the-brainbox look, and his grunted response wasn't hostile.

The plan was to leave at sundown when the town was occupied with feeding itself spiritually or gastronomically. An hour before, Charley and Matt took me into the freezing little shed we were using as a headquarters and we got down to the serious business.

'Here's your route to the river,' Charley said. He'd marked it in a thick red line on a standard survey map. 'You get over the mountains usin' the pass here.'

'Over?' I yelped. 'Over, in this weather?'

'Won't be too bad just yet. Eli's done it a hundred times. Just trust him.'

I thought of that crinkled face and trust wasn't the word that came to mind. 'Do you trust him?'

'Uh huh,' Charley grunted, suddenly sounding like an Indian himself. 'I do an' it's partly a matter o' blood kin. Now pay heed, Dick. Eli'll get you a canoe and you move down river, going east and south.' He traced the route with a wide, horny thumbnail.

'That's not just one river,' I said.

'Right,' Matt Tolliver slapped his thigh and produced a silver flask. He took a swig and re-corked it. 'Best to start off sober and stay that way. You're right about the river, less'n they've gone and cut canals through and I can't see how they could through that solid rock.'

'There's a little portin' to do, Dick,' Charley said.

'Porting?'

'Carryin' the canoe. By the time you get down there you won't need many provisions. The fish jus' jump out o' the water for one thing. You'll make out OK. Eli knows all about it.'

I lit a cigarette and wished Tolliver would produce the flask again but he didn't make a move. He was still suspicious of me, and doubtful, probably, but not as doubtful as I was myself. I blew smoke and tried to look unconcerned; I had no choice anyway as Charley had said. 'Fine. What happens after I leave the river and part company with Eli? Where's the bloody gold?'

Charley produced a pouch from his inside pocket. It was wrapped in oilskin and sealed with tape. A leather thong hung from the binding. 'It wouldn't do for you to be dwelling on the gold jus' yet, Dick. Wear this inside your shirt. Put the thingummy round your neck . . . that's right. What you've got there is a map and instructions to make you a rich man. Open it up when you get off the water. Like a reward.' He leaned closer to me and I could smell the aftereffects of the barbering he'd had that morning. I was conscious of my own rank smell and inferior status. 'An' don't let Eli see it,' he whispered.

Well, that was wonderful – I was to go off into the frozen wastes trusting my very life to a savage who would observe blood kin obligations so long as there wasn't any big money involved.

'You scared?' Matt Tolliver said.

'Yes.'

'Be a fool if you weren't.' He raised his flask to me in a silent toast.

Charley gave him a sour look and punched me encouragingly on the shoulder. Through the heavy shirt, sweater and lined coat I was wearing I could still feel the weight of the punch. 'In the pouch, Dick, you'll also find the details on how to find us once you're over the border. That parr'll be child's play.'

'What will you two do if I don't turn up?'

Matt turned away and spat out the window onto the cold hard ground. There was a light snow falling as the day died.

'Good cover, that snow,' Charley said.

'You haven't answered my question.'

'Don't hardly have to,' Matt said, 'because it doesn't make any sense. Where you're going there's only one way through. Eli'll see you make it till you get to this place. If you don't make it through it'll mean you're dead and Charley 'n' me'll come up here again and do the job ourselves. We've got a deal.'

Charley nodded. 'But we'll see you in Washington State, Dick.'

'Next year,' Tolliver added.

CHAPTER TWELVE

Wherever I am, on a beach, even in a sauna, I get cold when I think of that journey I made with Eli Hardpebble in the early winter of 1922. I've heard since that it was a particularly mild year without major storms and blizzards and of course we were heading away from the really cold zone. That's in theory. Because there was a fair amount of 'up' and considerable 'east' in it, and the going was harder and colder than any travel I ever experienced, before or since.

The company was part of the problem. The only thing Eli said for the first eight hours was, 'Snow cover tracks. Good.' That tended to be the style of his conversation in fact. He made practical observations and registered approval or disapproval of them. 'Big wind comin' up,' he might say. 'Bad.' I'd nod and prepare for more suffering.

I haven't the faintest idea of the route we took or even of the direction we travelled. Eli led the way with me spending as much time up on the back of the dog sled as I could. The practice I'd had with Fitzgerald stood me in good stead and I didn't disgrace myself although the dogs seemed to find it hard keeping up with Eli's tireless tread. The first night we made camp before dawn in the shelter of a big rock. Over the soup and bread I asked Eli how he was able to move so fast on the snow. He took a long slurp from his mug (his eating style was just a notch or two more civilised than that of the dogs), and pointed to his snow-shoes leaning against the rock.

'Big,' he said. 'Good.' He jutted his chin at my shoes which were much smaller.

'I know,' I said. 'Small. Bad.'

Eli nodded.

This was another one of young Fitzgerald's idiocies. The original Dawson Patrol had used small snow shoes for some reason and this had slowed them down. The nephew was determined again to prove uncle had been right. I've often wondered what happened to Fitzgerald II's patrol – probably had to be air-lifted out[17].

As we went higher the snow got thicker, the nights got colder and we had to pitch a tent each time we stopped. We ate the heavier food first, like the canned goods and the vegetables, and after a week it was a miserably tedious diet of rice, beans and salt meat. We carried fish and meat for the dogs and some nights Eli set snares for rabbits and hares. He wasn't always successful and there wasn't a lot of meat on the ones he caught, but it was welcome. We fed the bones and offal to the dogs.

The actual crossing of the mountains, even though it was through a pass and well below the peaks that towered above us, was arduous. I was either in a sweat of fear or a sweat of exertion or frozen to the marrow. If you think it's impossible to have a freezing cold prick you're wrong. Try marching through snowdrifts of the right depth, with soaking wet clothing and a sled in front of you pushing the snow and slush back, and you'll get the effect all right. I've often wondered if a woman could experience the corresponding discomfort but the topic has never come up. Women, on the whole, are too smart to walk hundreds of miles through ice and snow. The exceptions would be Eskimo and Indian women of course, but you don't talk about discomfort to an Indian woman. You stick to basic subjects like your own bravery, what's in the pot and who farted under the bearskins.

Which brings me to the second leg of the journey – on the rivers on the eastern side of the mountains. I was drawn fairly fine by the time we made the crossing. The food had run out for both dogs and men and there'd been no game for a couple of days. I'd had too little sleep, too much walking and not nearly enough whisky. Charley had forbidden us to pack any which turned out to be the right advice given the way Eli behaved later, but it seemed like a severe hardship at the time. A bad snowstorm, an injury to Eli or myself or an accident with the dogs and I'm sure I'd have left my bones on those mountains. It makes me cold to think of it . . . [Browning breaks off at this point, evidently to get himself a fresh bottle. The tape machine is turned off and when he resumes he appears not to have followed his usual practice of running the tape back to replay his last words. Consequently, he picks up the story somewhat in advance of where he left off. Ed.]

Eli traded the dogs, the sled and harness for a canoe and provisions. We also picked up some company, a small band of Kutchin. They were travelling in the same direction to meet up with some others who had been working for timber millers further south. Believe it or not, their intention was to head northeast to do some trapping.

'Won't they slow us down?' I asked Eli. The band consisted of two old men and one old woman plus four younger women with small children.

'Woman strong, carry canoe. Good.' Eli said.

If he meant carry *our* canoe I was all for it. The thing looked pretty heavy – stitched sections of hide stretched over a heavy wooden frame with solid ribs. The paddles were heavy too, and by the time we got it loaded, with our food, tent, groundsheets, guns and ammunition, I doubted my ability to lift it off the ground let alone carry it. Charley was right about the fish though. I could see them in the clear cold water, darting across the stony bottom and rising for insects. We might drown, but we wouldn't starve.

Before we took to the river I showed the map to Eli and tried to get him to indicate where we were. He stared at the sheet in puzzlement and when he turned it over to look at the other side I knew I wasn't going to learn anything useful this way. I was tempted to open the pouch, which I'd kept so close to my skin the whole way, that it smelled very bad. But Eli's eyes missed nothing and although he was silent most of the time I had the feeling that he knew exactly how much money I was carrying (not much) and how many bullets and shotgun shells I had (not many). I left the pouch alone.

The first few days were peaceable enough. I seem to remember four canoes but it might have been five. The able-bodied were distributed so that each of the Indians' canoes had at least one capable paddler. Our canoe had two – Eli and one of the young women. At first I was hopeless, dipping the thing in at the wrong time and nearly getting it wrenched from my hands by the current. This occasioned mirth among the savages, particularly Warm-Woman-With-Hot-Breath, the female in our canoe who had the ringside seat. After having her fun for a morning she crawled back from her position in the centre of the canoe to the stern where I was flailing away and showed me how it was done. There was a lot of wrist in it as I recall and a peculiar rhythm which she imparted to me by clicking her tongue. She was very close to me and her smell was distinctive. Shutting my eyes, I can bring it back now – a smoky odour with a nutty tang. Her breath *was* warm and not at all disagreeable.

At times the river was in shadow and it was very cold under the overhanging trees and high, rocky banks, but for long stretches we seemed to be heading directly into the sun and we had to peel off our heavy clothing and even mop our brows. The paddling was pretty hard work and you had to stay alert for currents, mudbanks and the like – it wasn't like punting on the Cam, I can tell you.

When she took off her buckskin overshirt and sat a couple of feet away from me in a red woollen shirt with her single braid hanging down her back and her brown arms plying the paddle like a conductor with his baton, Warm-Woman was the best looking creature around by a mile. She looked beautiful in fact, and Browning has always been an admirer of beauty. We made camp by the stream, cooked some fish the Indians had caught and stretched out in our blankets to smoke before sleeping. I couldn't get the woman out of my mind. I looked across to one of the other camp fires and there she was, looking at me.

It had been a long time since I'd touched a woman and, free of the Mounties, feeling fit and well and on my way to a fortune, I was in fine fettle and raring to go. Warm-Woman was giggling and looking at me. She'd whisper to her companions, look across the fire and giggle again. *You're in, Browning*, I thought, and I beckoned to her, holding up a cigarette I'd just rolled as an enticement. She whispered and giggled some more and then came around the fires and the sleeping old people to squat down beside me. She had a blanket wrapped around her but, as far as I could see, not much underneath it except the woollen shirt. She accepted the cigarette which I lit with a taper from the fire.

She held my hand as I lit the cigarette, just as a woman might in an LA singles bar, and I slid my fingers through her long, dark hair which was now unbraided and hanging loose. As I've said, I had a smattering of Kutchin which I'd learned from Sergeant Fraser and Eli and she had a little English which she'd picked up here and there. Since we both had the same thing on our minds, conversation wasn't really a problem as I recall, although it took some strange twists.

'You are beautiful,' I said, using one of the many Kutchin words for spring flowers (not that I knew them, but Fraser had told me this was the case) to get the idea across.

'You are so ugly,' she said.

'Eh?'

It turned out she meant I could be beautiful too but there were a few things in the way, notably hair. Your Indian males are almost hairless, you see, and the Indians put hairy people a little over towards the animal kingdom. But make no mistake, she could tell a man with the right equipment and intentions when she saw one and she wasn't about to let the opportunity pass by.

There was a deal of giggling along with some coffee drinking and tobacco smoking and the upshot was that she went to work on me with a pair of trade store scissors and cut-throat razor. The result was that, using the razor and a bit of fat and some hot water, she shaved me as smooth as a baby's bum. She also plucked my eyebrows and plaited my hair into a thick braid. When she'd finished she let me look at myself in a small mirror she carried in her bag of tricks. She'd stopped giggling. I looked and nearly fell into the fire: it had been a good while since I'd seen myself without hair on my face. With my head hair drawn back, with the squinting dark eyes and the flattened nose, I looked like an Indian.

I certainly passed muster with Warm-Woman. By word and gesture she got me to move my blankets a little way from Eli and the others. The fires were embers when Warm-Woman and I settled down. We had a few differences to get around. Kissing was a new thing to her but she picked it up pretty quickly, as I found out about certain kinds of biting. It was cold and we took off only the clothes we needed to and we had to keep several layers of wool and skin over us. It didn't matter: when it comes right down to it, everyone does it the same way. She was warm and smooth and had a muscular suppleness you don't find in civilised women. After some very interesting preliminaries, I was deep inside her and she was scatching my back and whimpering and I was plunging away and burying my face in the warm, smoky, nutty odour of her hair.

CHAPTER THIRTEEN

I have to admit river travel had some advantages over foot-slogging through the snow, but it wasn't all beer and skittles. When the weather was bad we got soaked through in the canoes and the wind seemed to freeze the water. Then there were the rapids – nasty stretches of white water where I shut my eyes and did what Eli and Warm-Woman told me to do and didn't look again until we were through. The portin', as Charley Moon had called it, wasn't too bad. We had to carry the canoes over short distances, to get around impossible barriers and to make a few changes of direction, but the Indians were experts at distributing the loads, sliding the boats and lowering them by rope so the work wasn't back-breaking.

The food was boring but plentiful and the nights were fun. Warm-Woman and I got along famously, mainly because we didn't have much to say to each other, nothing to fall out over, and we knew how to please each other under the blankets. I can't say I took much to Indians in general though. Eli seemed to get more sullen as the trip went on; some of the oldsters disapproved of what Warm-Woman and I were up to and made no bones about showing it. There was a certain amount of spitting more or less in my direction and once I'm sure I was given some rotten fish deliberately. I couldn't swear to it, but it was my firm belief that the time the canoe nearly dropped on me from twenty feet above, wasn't due to an accidental slip of the rope.

I never knew whether the Dawson City Mounties made enquiries about me or not. I suppose they did and they may have sent telegraph messages out on the subject, but I passed through a couple of Mountie-controlled river settlements without attracting any attention. I didn't give my mind to washing, I must admit, and my skin darkened with dirt and exposure. I kept my face shaved smooth, mainly because it pleased Warm-Woman, but also because it helped me to pass as a Kutchin or at least a half-breed of whom there were plenty around in those backblocks. We met people on the river – timber workers, prospectors and fishermen – and no one said boo to me.

I had no idea of distance and direction and had to rely on odd scraps of information I picked up, like overhearing conversations between the sort of people I've mentioned and the names of some of the tiny river hamlets we passed through. Most weren't marked on the map but a couple of the names fitted in – Fellows Hole might be a miserable collection of shacks not on the map but Fellows Falls, a drop in the river that required some porting, might be marked. From these clues I judged that we were making slow progress south-east.

But things started to feel uncomfortable – Eli was getting into pow-wows with the old men and one of the women attacked Warm-Woman over nothing at all. I tried to talk to Eli but got nowhere and Warm-Woman couldn't or wouldn't tell me what was going on. Under the strain, my thoughts began to drift to alcohol as they always have and that's what brought things to a head. We fetched up at a little place called Kennedy's Crossing where the river was wide and there were a few cabins, a logging camp and a ferry. The ferry was just a barge which was pulled across by a team of mules turning a kind of winch arrangement on either side. I was sorely in need of white companionship by this time, preferably accompanied by whisky and tobacco, and I wouldn't have minded a chance to try out some of Warm-Woman's biting tricks on a plump blonde either.

There was nothing like that in Kennedy's Crossing of course, but there was a small store and it did sell whisky.

The Indians didn't want to stop, naturally enough. The usual reception for them at such places was to have stones thrown at them or even a few shots fired at the canoes for sport. I persuaded them that I'd buy tobacco, of which we were running short, and even old sourpuss Eli could see the merit in that. We passed the settlement, tied up at a secure place by the bank and I walked back. I had my revolver tucked down inside my pants but there wasn't much else of Western civilisation about me. My hair was in a plait, I had a band around my head and Warm-Woman had done some fancy stitching on my jacket. I had a bone necklace around my throat and I wore leggings. I'd taken the precaution of crumpling and creasing the paper money I took with me and also of taking a fistful of coins. As I walked along the river I had two worries: would I make some sort of mistake and give myself away? and had Eli seen the pouch as I was putting the necklace on? I was pretty sure he had. No, I had three worries. Had Warm-Woman told Eli about the pouch? She'd have known about it for sure and he seemed to be looking at me very keenly as I was getting dressed.

'Breed?' This was the polite enquiry from the proprietor of the store in Kennedy's Crossing. He was a fat, bearded individual who smelled worse than any of the Indians. His store, which doubled as a bar and other things such as a rough laundry (and possibly a tannery as well, to judge from the stink), was just a big cabin with a stove and empty whisky boxes to sit on. The owner stood behind two barrels and did his business on their scarred and battered tops.

'Uh,' I grunted in the Kutchin manner and took out some money.

'What d'you want?'

Two men came into the store and walked over to the barrels.

'Breed here's got some dough,' the storeman said.

The two newcomers were timber men, to judge from their cleated boots and the smell of sawdust. 'Big buck, ain't he?' one of them said. 'Don't reckon as I've ever seen a breed as tall as him.'

The other put a coin on a barrel top. 'He sure is. Mean lookin' too. Give us two shots, Joe.'

That was where I almost made the sort of mistake I'd worried about. It goes against the grain for a man to stand and be discussed like a piece of horseflesh and to be butted in on as if he wasn't there at all. I *nearly* slammed my fist down and said something sharp about Canadian bad manners, but I'd spent time in country towns in Australia and I'd seen that the blacks and half-castes were treated like this. Their strategy seemed to be to let it run off them like rain, to stand and wait until they got what they wanted. It looked like I had to do the same.

Joe served the timber men who took their drinks across near the stove. 'Now,' he said, 'what d'you want?'

I used the Kutchin word and then corrected myself. 'Tobacco,' I said.

'Why, sure. You want Bull?'

I nodded and held up eight fingers. He put eight sacks of Bull Durham on the barrel.

'Whisky,' I said, keeping my voice low.

He shook his head. 'Sellin' whisky to Indians is a sure way to get unpopular around here. They get drunk, smash every durn thing in sight . . .'

I took back the paper money and most of the coins. Joe winked and nodded at me, a nasty sight because it caused the lock of greasy hair he wore pasted across his bald head to fall down over one eye. 'Lin'ment, you say? Why, sure thing, Chief. Couple bottles o' this and I guarantee there won't be a stiff joint in the whole tribe.' He gestured to me to put the money back and reached behind to a shelf. He pulled out three bottles of cheap rye whisky and wrapped them in sacking, taking care not to let the bottles clink. He put the tobacco and the wrapped bottles in a burlap bag and pushed it to me. Three quarts wasn't enough for the thirst I was building up but it looked like it was all I was going to get. I took the bag and he grabbed the money.

'Now, git!' he hissed.

I got. I'd paid probably double for the whisky and too much for the tobacco but that's the way it is when you're playing on the losing team. I took a few pulls on a bottle as I walked along the muddy track beside the river. The liquor put me in a thoughtful frame of mind. I was pretty sure that Eli and Warm-Woman were in cahoots and up to no good. It made me think that Eli was near the end of his job and trying to work out how to quit with the most advantage to himself. Maybe I was close to the parting of the ways but I had to know for sure.

Perhaps the contents of the pouch would tell me all I needed to know but I'd become almost suspicious about the pouch and I didn't want to open it until I had a plan of action worked out. I felt I couldn't risk opening it unless I had Eli off guard. And Eli *never* seemed to be off guard. I put the bottle back and heard it clink against another; that little sound gave me an idea.

The Indians had made a half camp – a small fire was burning and a couple of the old people were sleeping – but Eli, Warm-Woman and the other young women plus the children were ready to go on the river again if that's what was decided. I judged we were far enough from the settlement to risk what I had in mind. I took the tobacco out of the bag and gave a sack each to Eli and Warm-Woman and another for the others to share. Indians don't go in for gratitude all that much but their grunts were in the approving style.

'Anything to eat?' I asked Warm-Woman.

'Fish.'

This meant that they'd built the fire over rocks and were roasting the fish underneath. It tastes all right but I was sick of fish and wished I'd bought some food in Kennedy's Crossing.

'How far to the horses?' I asked. Eli knew what I meant. When we got to the horses he would go his way and I mine. But he just shrugged and looked up over the high pine trees into the cloudy sky. It was cold, threatening to snow, and the place where we were tied up was as good a camping ground as any. I took out the bottle of rye and had a drink. Eli reacted the way I hoped he would: his dark, slanted eyes almost disappeared in the puckered look of longing that came over his face. *Got you, you bastard*, I thought.

I took another drink. 'How far, Eli?'

'Not far. Whisky good.'

'How far? One day, two days?' I held the bottle as if I might give it to him if he answered. He took a stick and broke it in half. 'Half a day, eh?' I reached for a tin mug and poured him a small slug. 'This river? This way?' I pointed and gave him the mug. He tossed off the drink in one gulp.

'Red rock.' He held the mug out. I took it, poured again and made as if to drink from the mug myself. His eyes followed me hungrily.

'A red rock by the river?'

He nodded and I gave him the mug. Warm-Woman had a cigarette smoking between her lips and seemed uninterested in the conversation but I had a feeling that she was following every word. I passed her the bottle; she took a drink, gasped and drank again. There wasn't a lot left in the quart now which was the way I wanted it. I poured the rest for Eli and put the bottle casually back in the bag.

'I'm hungry,' I said.

Warm-Woman produced the fish, three big trout, and the old people woke up and everybody ate. I had a little coffee left from the original provisions and I brewed up a pot. Eli drank some but the other Indians weren't interested. They were all grunting and honking away among themselves and I knew enough of the language to know what they were talking about – firewater. After the meal

I went for a walk carrying my coffee mug and the burlap bag. I poured some of the strong, dark coffee into the empty whisky bottle and filled it with water.

The afternoon wore on and cleared a little. It was cold but I judged it wasn't going to snow. I walked back into the camp to see that they'd built up the fire and even laid in a stock of wood. That suited me. I staggered a little and took a big swig from one of the bottles of rotgut rye.

'Eli, ol' buddy, an' Warm-Woman, my darlin' girl, le's have us a party!' I tossed the opened bottle to Eli who caught it and handed the unopened one to one of the ancients who gave a whoop and tore at the cap with the couple of teeth he had left. I stumbled and fell down on a blanket near the fire.

Eli took a careful sip and handed the bottle to Warm-Woman. I reached into the bag, got the other bottle out, opened it and let the cold coffee-flavoured river water run down my throat.

CHAPTER FOURTEEN

Old and young, the Indians drank themselves into a stupor within a couple of hours. The children gave up yelling and trying to stir them to prepare food or anything else and crept into the blankets to huddle down with the snorers. Warm-Woman was one of the first to succumb, mainly because she took more drink on board than the others. Eli behaved just exactly as I thought he might. He got good and drunk; drunk enough to make him mean and brave but he didn't pass out. What he did was watch me.

As for me, I was the life of the party. When we were at the lively stage I was one of the liveliest. I did a war dance around the fire, stuck feathers in my hair and used the few Kutchin words about sex I knew, as loud and as often as I could. I got a few laughs and then everyone got bored with me and proceeded with their own drinking. What I *didn't* do was ever let go of my bottle. I kept it while I was dancing and while I was staggering off into the woods to piss.

It got dark early; Eli put more wood on the fire and filled his pipe. I swigged on my bottle, spilt some, made a cigarette and spilled that too. I swore and fell over. Then I crawled into my blankets and drew my knees up. I thrashed about for a while looking like I was trying to get comfortable – in fact I was getting a knife out of its sheaf and getting the long Colt into a position where it would do the most good. In my cavortings I'd managed to ensure that the rifle, shotgun, ammunition, matches and some beans were stowed in one canoe. The moon came up bright and clear over the trees and I lay still and started to snore.

If you've ever tried to pretend to snore for an hour you'll know that it's about as hard a thing as there is to do. My mouth dried out, my nose blocked and my head ached, but I kept it up until Eli was convinced and came sneaking over towards me. I could smell the whisky on him from a few yards away and I wouldn't have dared lie there like that if I hadn't thought that sobriety and the element of surprise would give me the edge. The old villain crept close and I saw moonlight glint on the blade of his knife. That brought me out in a sweat but his target wasn't my throat, not in the first instance anyway, but the thong around my neck which held the pouch. He was confident and a little sozzled; when he had his blade on the thong I made my move. I slipped my hand out from under the blankets and put the point of my knife into his crotch.

'Don't move a muscle, Eli, or I'll feed your balls to the fish.'

He froze and I took the knife from his hand. By the time he recovered I had the Colt cocked and under his chin. I was trembling which probably didn't help him feel any more secure. I pulled the pouch from inside my shirt.

'You wanted this?'

He nodded.

'Charley Moon tell you to get it?'

He shook his head. That had been one of my worries – that I had been set up in some way by Charley.

'Why, then?'

'Warm-Woman say much money in pouch.'

Well, she was right in a way of course, but just a little off the track. I tucked the pouch back and gestured for Eli to stand. He did and I got to my feet with the blanket still around my shoulders. We must have looked a sight standing there in the moonlight, with the pines casting long shadows, the camp fires burning low and the Indians sleeping like the dead. The real Indian and the make-believe

Indian: it would've made a good scene for the movies and they've probably done it, near enough, in some B Western or other. But it was no entertainment then; Eli would be dangerous as long as there was breath in his body and I didn't know what to do next or how to control him. Fortunately, he solved the problem himself by pulling out a knife he had hidden somewhere and leaping straight at me.

I didn't have time to think but I'd been right in my assessment of the situation – the liquor Eli had drunk had made him a less effective savage. He was a little slow and lop-sided in his leap and I had just enough space to swing the long Colt in and bring the barrel and some of my fist up hard against his temple. Eli dropped like a stone; he'd hadn't yelled when he'd attacked, probably because there was no other male Indian to show off to, so the rest of the band slept on. I stood there with a bruised knuckle and a heaving chest and wondered if I'd ever walk down a civilised street and sleep under a roof and in a proper bed again.

But there wasn't much time for philosophising. Eli could wake up at any moment and so might Warm-Woman. There was no telling what she might do if she saw me and my pouch slipping away – a well-thrown hatchet wouldn't have been beyond her. I grabbed my blankets and a fur rug and crept to the river bank. Into the canoe went the bedding and as many of the paddles as I could find. I used my knife to hole the other canoes – not enough to ruin them but enough to need patching and prevent pursuit. Doing all this, plus untying the canoe in the dark was tricky work and I suppose I made enough noise to waken the Indians if they hadn't been full of whisky.

My feet were wet, I was sweating and I'd skinned my knuckles, but at last I was in the canoe with the load properly distributed and a couple of feet of water underneath me. I dipped the paddle and manoeuvred out into mid-stream. The black water flowed quietly, which wasn't to say that around the bend there couldn't be a hellish stretch of rapids or a waterfall or a fork in the river with no signpost.

It's a bad habit of mine to expect the worst when I'm in physical danger and the best when the danger appears to be past. It hasn't always worked out like that. I drew a breath and looked up past the high, dark pines to the clear sky. A light breeze was moving the tops of the trees but the air was cold and still on the water. I took one look back at the bank; I could just see the glow of the fire. I had a flash of regret for the warm, musty feel of the Indian woman who was one of the most comfortable bed companions I've ever had. I'd never paddled one of the canoes solo until then, but I'd never beaten an Indian with a knife or drunk a whole bottle of coffee-flavoured water either – there's a first time for everything. I dug into the water and headed off for the red rock, whatever the hell that was.

The next part of the journey was a piece of cake. If I'd managed to bring another bottle of whisky along to keep out the cold I'd have been almost happy. The river ran steadily; there was the occasional log to watch out for but no white water or forks. The moon cast enough light to keep the banks in sight and to avoid overhanging branches when the stream narrowed. I paddled for a couple of hours, then I tied up, slept fitfully until dawn, and set off again.

The sun was barely up when I rounded a bend and saw the red rock. Whether it would have been red at any other time of the day I'm not sure but it was certainly red then. It was a big lump of sandstone about thirty feet high jutting straight up above the river. Water had cut away the base and bushes had grown around the top but there was a flat face of a couple of hundred square feet and it glowed red in the dawn sun.

'Browning's luck,' I breathed, and I remember that the words came out with puffs of steam. It was bitterly cold. I pulled over to the bank beneath the rock, grabbed some branches and pulled in until the canoe was touching the bank. I tied up and climbed out onto the roots of some big trees that grew right to the water's edge. Ten minutes later I was at the base of the rock, twenty feet from the water and crouched over a fire and the coffee pot. I drank some scalding coffee, ate some jerky, smoked a cigarette, warmed my hands and opened the pouch. Inside was a map, some money and a note from Matthew Tolliver:

Hank (this was crossed out and 'Dick' written above it) –

Your on the Tusk river by red rock if you ain't in hell. In back of the rock you'll find a track witch leads to a road witch takes you to a farm. Bout a mile from the river. 25 years back the people on the farm was shit poor and i don't reckon things will have changed much. We bought some horses and you can do the same only don't get a bad one like pore 'Fancy' done, i hope you know horses. Won't none of them be good but don't get the worst is all i'm saying. Ask the farm folks to point you to Hanging Bluff but don't nessessarily believe what they tells you. Look at this map and find yore own way. If you was in the army the way Bob says you was you won't have any trouble.

Take a day's hard riding to Hanging Bluff two if you ain't a good rider or get lost or something. Just past the Bluff Fancy come off his horse and we walked back. He berried his gold deep under a big rock fifty paces due west of the Bluff. You can take a baring on a tree witch gives the Bluff its name. If the tree ain't there or if the creek's rose or changed direction or a badger's rooted up the bags you could have some trouble. If you find the gold you should ride south east til you get to the scarpment. Youl have to go threw a narrew george that will be icy this time of year and not easy, when yore threw line yourself up with the dip in the scarpment and you should be by a stream with some low hills to the east. Light a fire at dawn and send up a smoke of some kind, any kind will do. Fire two shots – rifel would be best but pistil will do.

This here's the longest letter I ever writ and it's dang hard work to do it. I'd a sight rather make the trip yore on but Bob says we're

too old. I don't think so. fire the shots and wait. God wiling we'll be
seeing you soon. good luck.

The letter was written in ink with many blotches and crossings out.
I'm reading from it now as best I can because the paper is creased and
torn in places. The signature was very clear – Ollie Fisher Esq. God
knows where the old bandit picked up the 'Esq.' idea from. [Unlike
the other letter mentioned in this narrative, this from 'Ollie Fisher'
also known as Matthew Tolliver, has survived. Among Browning's
effects deposited in the Silkstein Agency basement, I discovered an
old leather pouch wrapped in dried out and dilapidated oilskin. The
letter was inside the pouch which identifies it as the one Browning
wore around his neck on his Canadian journey. There was, however,
no trace of the map mentioned below. Ed.]

I examined the map and it seemed clear enough. The main features of the country – streams, high hills, distinctive rocks, etc. –
were marked and there were even suggestions as to the best places
to take shelter if the weather was bad. It was cold but not snowing
and the sky was a clear pale blue. There didn't seem to be any point
in delaying; the weather wouldn't get any better. I got the shotgun
from the canoe and put it over my back in a sling. I had a knife and
a pistol in my belt and a rifle under my arm; otherwise, I had only
a couple of rolled blankets, some dried meat, tobacco and matches,
along with some coffee and a tin pan in a soft Indian bag. Before I
left the river I hacked off my long hair with the knife and tried to
saw it into some kind of ordinary shape. My stubble had grown. I
ripped the fancy stitching off my coat and got rid of the bone necklace. With my pants worn out over the leggings I didn't look like a
half-breed anymore. Armed like that and smelling the way I must
have, I suppose I looked like a bandit or maybe a nervous prospector.
I tucked the note, map and money back inside the pouch and set off
along the track which was overgrown but followable. I was glad to
be walking again and exercising joints and muscles that had grown

stiff with all the canoeing. Being on horseback would be even better. I was reasonably confident although one thing worried me – Ollie hadn't said what I was to do if I *didn't* find the gold.

The people at the farm didn't seem surprised when I ambled in asking if I could buy a horse. Their spokesman was a tall, lean character with a spade beard who said his name was Brother Rivers.

'Well, Brother Rivers,' I said. 'How about you invite me in for a cup of coffee and we can horse trade.'

'I can't invite thee in,' he said. 'Thou art unclean.'

'Well, I haven't had much of a chance . . .'

'I mean spiritually. And we do not use coffee or engage in trade.'

'I see.' A few more had drifted into the yard outside the big log cabin and it didn't take much observation to see that this was some kind of religious community. There were more women than men for one thing which is something you'll always find in these set-ups. I've spent enough time in California to know – highly convenient arrangement for the men I've always thought, but I daresay the Bible gives it the okay somewhere. Ollie had been right though – they were shit poor to judge from their broken boots, threadbare clothes and starved look, and I'm talking about men, women and children.

'We are the Brethren of the Valley,' Brother Rivers said and a sigh escaped from the assembly. 'You come among us armed. You may take anything you want. That is our way.'

'No, no. I'm happy to pay.' I reached into the pouch and took out two ten dollar notes.

'We have no use for your money. Take anything.'

I glanced around. There wasn't much to take and I certainly didn't fancy any of the women. As to horseflesh, I couldn't see any unless you counted half a dozen mules pulling at grass around the base of one of the cabin walls. Just then a woman stepped from behind Brother Rivers. She was nearly as tall as he – a great raw-boned creature with a face like a gravestone and huge red hands dangling at the end of scrawny arms.

'We need the money, Brother. Take it. Let him have a mule.'

'Two mules,' I said.

'No. It is not our way!'

'It's not my way to let my children starve.' She reached over and took the twenty. Brother Rivers fell to his knees in the mud, turned his beard up to the sky and began to pray. The woman nodded to me and I walked over to the mules. They were ugly but strong-looking. I'd had some dealings with mules in the army and I knew that they'd sometimes get you through where your 'three parts thoroughbred at least'[18] would let you down.

'Have you got a saddle or anything?' I asked the woman.

She shook her head. 'Got a bit and rein you can have and some rope. You'll have to use your blankets.'

I nodded and gave her a silver dollar when she brought the harness. I picked out the two best-looking animals and tied a blanket around the one and strapped on the Winchester, shotgun and my bag. I put a lead rope on the other. Brother Rivers was still praying but the others were ignoring him and clustering around the woman with the money. I climbed up onto the mule, trotted around the yard once to get the feel of it and stopped near the woman.

'Can you tell me how to get to Hanging Bluff?'

She pointed south.

'Hard road?'

'Life is a hard road,' Brother Rivers said, 'for the ungodly.'

'You said it.' I touched my hand to my cap and the woman smiled at me. Scrubbed up, dressed properly and given a couple of years rest from hard labour, she mightn't have looked too bad.

'The road's all right. What're you looking for, stranger?'

'Gold,' I said.

Her laughter followed me out of the yard.

CHAPTER FIFTEEN

It started to snow on the ride to Hanging Bluff and I wished I'd brought the fur rug, but I'd wanted to put all things Indian behind me, I guess. My coat was lined and thick and I had good gloves but I was a bit cold around the head, and after a while the sun on the snow began to dazzle me, so that it was hard for me to keep direction and steer by the landmarks on Ollie's map. The mules were smart animals though: it was almost as if they knew what south meant. Many times I would've lost the direction but for the preference of the mule I was riding for one way around an obstacle rather than another.

I made good progress that day, covering about three quarters of the distance to judge from the map. I camped under a rocky cliff overhang which Ollie had marked as 'shalter'. As light snow had accumulated in the hollows, water was no problem. The country was lightly grassed and wooded and I had no trouble getting enough fuel for an all-night fire. However, it was hard to warm the body all round; only the part that faced the fire was really warm and I spent the night twisting and turning in my blankets. Coffee and dry meat aren't very warming either – I'd have given a lot of what money I had, something shy of a hundred dollars from recollection, for a bottle of whisky.

I'd hobbled the mules and they grazed contentedly enough. I was stiff and sore from the unaccustomed riding – a mule has a hard, narrow back – and the restless night. A mug of coffee, a cigarette and a thunderous bowel movement and I was ready to go on.

Overnight the snow had melted leaving the ground muddy but firm enough. The day was fine but I'd learned that the high, powdery clouds in the morning meant snow in the afternoon so I was keen to move fast.

Because of the hardship later, it now seems to me that the location of Hanging Bluff and the discovery of the gold was a piece of cake. You couldn't miss the Bluff. It was a high, rocky outcrop with a single tree growing on it. The tree had a thick branch running almost parallel to the ground about twelve feet up. It wasn't my imagination – I could see where ropes had scarred the branch. I was so excited when I dismounted that I almost forget to tether the mules and it still makes my blood run cold to think what would have happened if they'd run away. But I got them tied and checked Ollie's note again and took the fifty paces in the right direction. The creek hadn't risen, the boulder hadn't been disturbed and, after half an hour's scrabbling the dirt with my hands, the tin pan and a lump of wood, I dragged out two calico bags which had been wrapped in oilskin and were as sound as the day they were buried.

The bags weighed about fifty pounds each which would be a cruel weight to carry in that country on foot and would have taxed a horse already carrying a man and a similar load. I felt I should have been able to mark the moment at which I made my fortune with something more memorable than a chew on some jerky and a cigarette. But that was all I had and all the time I could spare. It was late morning and the clouds were beginning to take on a snowy look.

'Here's some work for you to do, Fraser,' I said to the pack mule. The animal stood docilely while I tied the bags securely on its back, one on each side. Suddenly I was a man of wealth and I felt the responsibility. I wanted an armed guard and a bulletproof vest but all I could do in the way of extra security was to sling the shotgun over my back again. I decided to call the other mule Pedro, after my old Mexico and Hollywood comrade Pedro Cortez, not that Pedro was a mule – far from it. I had thoughts of how to spend the money as I trotted south. Nothing exotic, nothing beyond a few gallons of champagne daily and a blonde with plenty of imagination.

I was happily lulled by these thoughts and Pedro's bumpy gait and so unprepared for the first sharp flurry of snow which happened almost at the entrance to Ollie's 'george'. I was in heavy timber following a faint track and with almost no view of the sky or what lay ahead above the tall pines. I still have nightmares about that place. I wake up sweating and yelling; I believe I'm stumbling along that ribbon of a track high up above razor-sharp rocks, blinded by snow and with my ears and nose about to drop off from cold. I don't know how it got that way, some freak of nature I suppose, but it seemed to trap icy winds and increase their velocity and drop their temperature until it seemed that nothing could live there. No vegetation did – from the first yard to the last it was a barren, stony stretch that wound and climbed and turned back on itself.

I've never bothered to study the geography of the place, but I think an underground river must have surfaced and cut the gorge through soft rock. I could hear water running below the track along the side of the almost sheer cliff but I couldn't see it down through the snow and mist. There was no water at the other end so I guess the river must have gone underground again. As I inched along on the mule, holding the lead rope and feeling for the cliff wall to the right, I thought the gorge was bottomless and endless. It took hours and it was everything Ollie had said – icy in places so that I had to get down and lead the mules – and rock strewn. I heard occasional rumblings on the cliff but, mercifully, no rocks fell in my path.

Everything else happened though – I lost a glove heaving a big rock out of the way and Fraser snapped at my shoulder when I lurched against him. I felt the teeth go into my skin through the layers of clothing and I yelled. The shout echoed in the chasm, sounding high-pitched and panicky.

'God,' I yelled, 'what am I doing here?'

'Do-ing he-yah?' the mountain wailed back at me.

I was ready to stop, lie down and die, when the mist ahead suddenly lifted. I could see the path and it was twice as wide as it had been. I plodded on and saw a clump of grass. The mules whinnied and trotted forward. The ground sloped gently down and the path broadened. I whooped and Pedro cantered if that's the right word for a mule. I had no feeling in my right hand, my feet or in my nose and ears but I could smell and taste forest and grass. After a hundred yards I pulled Pedro up, slid off and let the animals graze while I made a fire. The coffee and tobacco were about the best I ever tasted.

Looking back I could see that the gorge had cut through a narrow range of what you might call hills if you were flying over them but what had seemed like mountains to me. There was snow on the higher reaches and not much timber. A few miles ahead there was another similar range which looked blue in the distance. I was in a sort of oasis of flat, mild country between two stretches of heartbreak. I considered turning west, towards where I took the coast to be but for all I knew the flat land could give way to more mountains in that direction.

'No choice for it, Dick,' I said out loud. 'You have to trust Matt Tolliver and Coldknife. At least they haven't lied to you so far about how horrible everything would be.'

The mules looked at me as I spoke. They were red-eyed with the cold but they'd eaten well and weren't too heavily laden. I'd lost a lot of weight, I realised, and no wonder. I put my hands on my middle where I'm apt to carry a bit of flesh when I'm eating and drinking well and felt just muscle and bone.

'A hundred and sixty pounds at the most,' I said. 'A bloody middleweight.'

The mules moved nervously. I inspected my shoulder where Fraser had snapped at me and found torn cloth and clotted blood.

'You bastard,' I said. 'Just like your namesake.'

I cleaned up the camp, mounted and headed for the hills. Within half an hour I spotted the dip in the otherwise straight line of the escarpment ahead. But I was still travelling on the flat and it was almost an hour before I had low hills to the side of me the way Ollie's note directed. I suppose I kept putting the moment off. I dismounted, made a fire keeping it virtually smokeless and drank coffee and smoked. I was still shaken by the experience in the gorge and a little light-headed.

'You'd have to be a fool to trust those bandits,' I said.

Pedro pricked up his ears and whinnied.

'But what else can you do? You're lost, you haven't any food and your shoulder's infected.'

I suddenly realised that this was true. My shoulder was throbbing painfully and I fancied I was running a fever. One of my rules has always been to get medical treatment the instant something ails me. It's kept me alive these many years; not because I believe the doctors actually do any good, but because it sets the mind at rest and shifts the worry on to others. I always feel better when other people are worrying about me, means I worry less myself. I built up the fire, threw some green branches on it and sent big clouds of thick smoke up into the sky. I waited an hour and then fired my rifle three times into the air.

That was a mistake. The mules screeched and ran. I turned and saw them bolting across the plain back towards the gorge but I was too weak to chase them. I didn't like to do it but I had no choice; I dropped to one knee, sighted and brought Fraser down with one shot. I sighted on Pedro but this time I couldn't do it. He was a tough, game animal and I wasn't going to shoot him for the sake of a blanket, a bridle and a bit of rope. I watched while he skittered into a line of trees, came out again and then disappeared behind a rise.

Fraser was thrashing on the ground a hundred yards away. I hurried to him and put a bullet in his head. He was heavy and I had to strain every muscle to get one of the bags out from under him. I made it eventually with my shoulder aching fiercely and a trembling feeling in my legs. I carried the hundred pounds of gold back to my camp fire which was still sending up thick smoke.

Flopping down on the grass I felt the first flakes of snow.

'Oh, no,' I groaned.

'You sure are a sorry sight.'

I swung around and pointed the Winchester at the chest of the man who had stepped out of the timber behind me. It was an easy chest to aim at as it must have been as wide as a side of beef and its owner stood closer to seven feet than six. I couldn't have failed to hit him somewhere.

'Welcome back to the USA, son,' he said.

'What?'

'You don't need the rifle, boy. I'm Mike Flood. Old Matt Tolliver sent me.'

CHAPTER SIXTEEN

Mike Flood kicked out the fire with his huge buckskin boots and picked up the gold sacks, one in each hand, as if they were bags of candy.

'Hey,' I yelped, 'they're mine.'

'No, they ain't. They belong to Matt and to Coldknife.'

'We're partners.'

'So 'm I, in a way. Bit I ain't about to go around claiming this gold as mine.'

'Well, I meant . . .'

'Let's go and get warm. I'll bet you could do with a drink.'

There were no better words to get me going. I tramped along after Flood through the light timber towards the escarpment. Flood was one of those men who always seem to have you at a disadvantage. Here was I, with a rifle and shotgun and a pistol in my belt while he had a fifty pound bag in each hand, and still I felt he could do with me what he liked. Maybe it's a weakness in me.

As we walked, Flood explained to me how Ollie and Charley had set things up. Flood was on stand by in Everett, a small town just inside the US border. Charley sent a wire from Dawson when I started out and Flood trekked inland from Everett to set up a waiting post near where I'd cross the border. He had a cabin about an hour's march from the place where I was scheduled to send up the smoke. So here we were.

'There were a lot of things to go wrong,' I said. 'How long were you supposed to wait for me?'

'Weather gets real bad here in February. If'n you weren't here by late this month, wouldn't be much point in waiting.'

'How long have you looking for the smoke.'

'Coupla weeks, sort of. Only this last few days for real. You made pretty good time.'

'That must have been a round the clock job.'

He turned and looked at me. 'Well, I didn't think you'd be dumb enough to send up smoke at night. Figured you'd use the daylight hours which, as you may have noticed, ain't all that long just now. If'n you'd been dumb enough to try it at night you'd have been too dumb to get through. Charley opined you weren't that dumb.'

We marched on for a while with me digesting the information and trying to keep up. The track was narrow and rough and inclining upward. I hoped we weren't heading for the escarpment, dip or no dip.

'We're not going to cross those hills, are we?' I panted.

'Hell, no. Ain't you got no eye for country? Those hills're a coupla hours away. You think I coulda made from there to where you were in an hour?'

'I suppose not.'

'Not unless I could fly.' This made him laugh; he almost stumbled because he was laughing so hard.

'What's funny?'

'You'll see.'

'One other thing bothers me, er . . . Mike.'

'What's that?'

'I mean, in terms of things that could've gone wrong with Charley and Ollie's plans. What if I'd got through but without the gold?'

'No problem,' Flood said. 'Not much cash for me but my instructions in that unhappy event were just to shoot you. I'd say that shot of yours that brought down the mule kinda saved your life. You're a lucky feller.'

I wasn't feeling very lucky. It got colder as we climbed and I felt sure that snow was not far off. I was drained physically and emotionally and not in any shape to cope with hardship. I told Flood a little about my journey, particularly about Eli's treachery.

'Yes, well, old Eli Hardpebble, he's getting on in years. He'd be looking for a little something to put by him same as me 'n' others. 'Course, at your age, it don't seem so pressing.'

This wasn't comforting. I've got nothing against old-timers getting together a nest egg but not at the expense of young men that have to make their way. After nearly an hour's walking Flood stopped and wiped his sweating face.

'Are we there? I don't see a cabin.'

'Not yet, close.' He put the gold down and looked at me. I couldn't see any weapons about him but you can never be sure. I put my hand on the pistol butt, not sure that I could pull it out and fire it quick enough to stop him if he wanted to come at me. He didn't seem to notice.

'Darn me, Hank. That's your name, ain't it?'

'It'll do.'

'Not as young as I was. I figured we'd have an animal to bring us back or at least pack the gold. Didn't reckon on you losing *two* beasts. That'll make a story for Matt 'n' Bob.'

'Will they be coming here?'

He laughed that great, gusty laugh again and bent down to pick up the bags. 'No, not here. We'll be seeing them in Chicago.'

And that's what happened. We went back to Flood's cabin, rested, fed and got drunk. Floyd rubbed bear grease into my bruised and bitten shoulder and bound it up tight. We set off the next day for Seattle. We spent a night in Seattle, long enough to buy some clothes, get drunk again and sober up slowly with hot towels on my face as I got properly barbered. Then we boarded a train going east. I don't remember much about the journey apart from the comfort. Flood booked us first class and we travelled in a heated compartment, ate and drank well and slept warm at night. My shoulder mended fast. It was my first taste of the good life since leaving California in the fall of the previous year, and I revelled in it, tipping the Pullman attendants and buying flowers at the stops for every woman that took my eye.

Everyone seemed very prosperous but that was probably because we were travelling high on the hog ourselves. I've noticed that when you're in funds you don't seem to see the poor people but the reverse isn't true – when you're poor all you can see is the rich. Flood was pretty good company. He'd been a bandit back in the Soapy Smith days with Tolliver and Coldknife and he made no bones about it.

'Ollie told me that they didn't kill anyone in the holdup,' I said. I was lighting a cigar and turning it in the flame.

'That's right. They never killed anyone deliberate-like that I ever heard of.'

I showed him the posters which I'd kept through all my trials and tribulations. He looked at them and nodded. 'They had a lot of accidents,' he said.

Flood kept a close watch on the gold and wouldn't let me carry a gun. He made me leave the Winchester '78 behind and stow the long Colt and the shotgun, which had a detachable stock, in the baggage. He carried a Smith & Wesson revolver which he handled confidently. Otherwise I felt fairly relaxed with him; he'd had a dozen opportunities to kill me and had never made a move. The only thing I had against him was that he won too much of my money at poker.

After London, Chicago was the biggest city I'd seen up to that time and it was by far the busiest. Everybody seemed to be going places on the run; the traffic rushed down the streets and the trolley cars shrieked when they stopped as if they couldn't wait to get going again. Just walking along a street, particularly on the West

Side where Flood and I installed ourselves in a hotel, you could see specimens of every race in the world. Flood pointed this out to me as he looked from the window down to the street.

'I've seen yids, niggers, chinks, dagoes, injuns and I don't know what-all and I've only been looking a minute. Where you from, Hank? You a Canuk?'

'No, Australian.'

'How come you ain't black then?'

'We Australians turn white when we leave Australia. Haven't you ever heard of the White Australia policy?'[19]

He scratched his head. 'Seems to me I have. Well, fancy that now. I wonder anybody stays there. Who'd stay a nigger if'n he could change to a white man? Say, can you throw a boomerang?'

'Sure, if there was anywhere to throw it. This city's so tight-packed you can hardly get into full stride. How big is it?'

'Search me. But it's big enough to sell a hundred pounds of gold in and not cause no fuss.'

'And when does that happen? I'm anxious to be rich.' I knew Flood had spent some time in the telegraph office but he hadn't taken me into his confidence.

'Ain't we all. Happens the day after tomorrow, when the man flies in.'

'Flies?'

'Yup. Matt believes in moving with the times. The buyer comes in from Buffalo on Wednesday by plane. He pays up and flies out.'

'What about Ollie and Charley?'

'Darn confusing, you calling them that, but they fly in from Spokane about noon the same day. After they get the money they go south.'

'What about you?'

'I'm getting me a Buick and two or four women and some whisky and I'm heading where the fancy takes me. What'll you do, Hank?'

I realised then that I hadn't the remotest idea. The whole thing hadn't been real to me from Dawson City to this moment. But now it was. Airplanes, buyers, Buicks and women – these were the real things of life, not snow-shoes and Indians and swaybacked mules. I joined Flood at the window and looked down on the street. A woman came into view walking a small dog on a leash. The dog was wearing a plaid coat and the woman was tall and slim inside a below-the-knee fur coat with a nipped in waist and wide shoulders. Her hat was fur too, a tall, turbanlike affair; she had fine chiselled features and an arrogant, strutting walk. I thought of the things I had to do – re-establish an identity, discover how the land lay in California, maybe even check on my marital status and family prospects in Australia. The woman stopped and cocked a hand on her hip while the dog shat in the gutter.

'I think I'll stay right here for a while,' I said.

'Ain't a bad town,' Flood said. 'A mite dangerous, though.'

Coming from someone who'd thought nothing of risking his neck in those northern woods with an armed man carrying a fortune in gold and winter coming on, this opinion seemed worth attention but all Flood could tell me was that there were bootleggers around.

'Hell,' I said. 'We had them in Los Angeles, did a little business with them myself.'

'That so?' Flood seemed unimpressed and I took offence and didn't ask for more information. In the movies, men locked up together for a stretch of time, waiting for something, like a hanging or the arrival of a woman, draw close and tell each other their life histories. In my experience this is baloney; you tend to close up and withdraw, certainly you get tired of playing cards and all the other ways of passing the time. Result was that Flood and I were pretty on edge with each other by the time we were due to meet the buyer from Buffalo.

'Take the bags, Hank.' Flood had transferred the gold into two leather bags like small suitcases with straps and a strong lock. He tossed one across to me as if it was a football.

'Oof. What about you?'

'I've got the gun.'

Flood had rented a car and we drove about twenty miles out of town to an airfield that looked as if it had been a potato patch until very recently. It was a cold grey day with the sun struggling to get through the clouds. There had been snow the night before and there was a thin scattering of it around the paddock. We parked beside an army surplus shed; Flood put the bags containing the gold inside the shed. We lit cigarettes and waited.

I didn't know it then but the aircraft the buyer arrived in was a De Haviland DH-4A, a solid-looking thing it was, with firm upright wing struts, a striped tail and substantial wheels. I speak as one who has learned to hate airplanes of all shapes and sizes, but especially fragile ones. The buyer, wrapped up in a camelhair coat, was a small man with a big moustache. He didn't give his name, just nodded to Flood and went into the shed. His pilot made some adjustments on the plane, checked his watch and looked up into the pale sky as the high drone of an approaching plane was heard. The pilot took a Thompson gun from his cabin and waited.

It was a Vickers Vimy, a converted bomber, with a wide wing span and two motors. Seeing Ollie and Charley climb down from this big plane was a strange experience. At that time the planes generally looked more fragile than the men if you follow me, but the two oldsters looked less solid than their aircraft. I *had* seen this sort of plane before during the war although I didn't know its name then. Charley pushed back his pilot's goggles and waved. Ollie was less enthusiastic; he busied himself with an attaché case and seemed to be trying to get himself warm. Again it was something I didn't then know, but it was cold flying in one of those open planes at a few thousand feet, even for an old Yukon hand. They nodded at the pilot and all three came across the landing field towards Flood and me. The pilot had his Thompson and Ollie and Charley both wore leather coats that bulged suspiciously. Flood had his revolver and the buyer probably had something; I was unarmed and very nervous. I tried not to show it and when Charley punched me on the shoulder I stood firm and punched him back.

'How'd you like the trip, Dick?' he bellowed, probably because he was deafened by the engine noise.

'It was hell,' I said. 'Oh, bits of the canoeing were all right.'

He said something to me in the Han language, something obscene to do with bear skins and I responded automatically. Charley laughed and turned to Ollie. 'He did all right, didn't he?'

Ollie nodded. 'Let's see how we do. Mike, you and Browning and the fly boy can wait here.'

'Browning?' Flood said.

'The Aussie, that's his name. Leastways, he says it is.'

'Aussie?' The pilot almost dropped his Thompson in surprise. 'You Australian? So'm I. Bluey Tait, pleased to meetcha. Browning, was it?'

I shook hands with him cautiously. 'Dick Browning,' I said. 'How're you going, Blue?'

'Blue?' said Flood. 'What sorta name's that?' He was peeved at being left out of the last stage of the deal.

'Can't you see his red hair?'[20] I said. Tait's deep red mop was visible under his cap.

'I don't get it,' Flood said.

While the men inside the shed did their business and Flood sulked, I chatted with Tait. He'd flown in the RAF during the war so I had to tread cautiously in exchanging war reminiscences. Luckily he was more interested in his own exploits than anything else, so he didn't notice my vagueness about battalions and battles. After a while the buyer and the old bandits came out, all smiling. The buyer nodded to Tait and strode towards his plane.

'See you, Dick,' Tait said. 'There's a bar on South Clark Street, the Spitfire, I drink there when I'm in town. Leave a message there and I'll get in touch. We'll have a beer.'

'Righto, Blue.'

We watched while Tait turned his plane, taxied and took off. Charley handed thick envelopes to Flood and me. Ollie had unscrewed the top of a silver flask. He took a swig and handed the flask to Flood.

'Drink up, Mike. A good bit o' business.'

Flood drank. 'What's my end?'

'Twenty four grand. Same for Dick. Have a drink, Dick.'

I did. I was stunned. It was more money than I'd ever had before. Mind you, I'd earned it. I took my turn at the flask which contained first grade bourbon.

'Well, Dick,' Charley said, 'those Mounties sure took it hard when you left. Have any trouble with old Eli?'

'Yes,' I said.

'Figured you would, but he was the man to get you through. Any complaints now?'

'No, but I have got a question. Why did you go to all that trouble to recruit someone up in the Yukon? Why didn't you just send someone in from the American side? Someone like Mike could've gone in and got that gold much easier than I did.'

Charley took a long drink and wiped his whiskers with the back of his hand. 'Thought about it, but it wouldn'a worked. If we'd sent someone in from the American side he'd have known where he was when he got the gold and how to handle the country. He coulda taken off in any direction. We needed someone like you – a regular babe in the wood.'

'But after Mike found me he could've taken off with the gold.'

'I figured you'd stop him. After what you'd been through you wouldn't be about to let one man rob you.'

That's where he was wrong, of course. Flood could've taken the lot, probably. But then again, I might have been angry enough to *try* to stop him. I'm just glad I didn't have to try.

'Time to go, Bob,' Ollie said quietly, 'and lay off that stuff. You gotta fly us outa here.'

Charley grinned at me, shook Flood's hand and mine and strolled back to the plane. Ollie took a deep drink from the flask, capped it and put it in his pocket where I heard it clink against metal.

'So long, Matt,' Flood said.

The bourbon was warm in my stomach and I drew deep on a Fatima as I watched the big bi-plane bounce across the field and sail up into the sky. It circled the field and then headed off towards the south; first the sound receded and then the plane was a diminishing speck among the clouds.

Flood felt the envelope bulging inside his coat pocket, slapped his hands and rubbed them together. 'Time to howl!'

'Yes,' I said. 'Time to howl!'

CHAPTER SEVENTEEN

I never saw Matt Tolliver, Coldknife Bob Carter or Mike Flood again after that day at the airfield, but a man with a sporting disposition and twenty four thousand dollars to spend doesn't lack for appreciative company. After all the privations and terrors I'd been through I was ready to howl, as Flood put it, and howl is what I did. Chicago was the place in which to have a good time in the 1920s and I should know because the good time I had practically put me in the grave.

For one thing, the Volstead Act had never been taken seriously in the Windy City. Certainly not by the Mayor, Big Bill Thompson, who ran the place for the first few years the Act was in force. The bars and cabarets were open around the clock, the old hands told me, and even when I first dipped my finger into the Chicago fleshpots in 1923, Prohibition was a joke. There was an honest Mayor by this time. I forget his name,[21] but sixty per cent of the cops were in the pay of the bootleggers and a goodly percentage of the politicians and judges were in the same boat. Anyway, most of them were such good customers they wouldn't want to see a single bottle broken. So one man's honesty didn't do anyone much good, or harm, depending on the way you looked at it.

I took an apartment in the Blackstone Hotel, spent a big wad on clothes and an even bigger one on a yellow Studebaker and proceded to hit the high spots. I called myself Richard Kelly, grew a neat moustache, and tried to forget Australia, and Douglas Fairbanks, and bootleggers and the Mounties and all the other individuals and organisations that had done me wrong. [Browning rambles a little at this point and only odd words, such as Dudleigh Grammar . . . bloody army . . . Billy Hughes[22] . . . can be discerned. The tape stops and Browning evidently resumed in a more coherent frame of mind some time later. Ed.]

Minette Kirby really taught me the Chicago ropes. She was a singer in the Midnight Reveille, a cabaret on Diversey Street on the North Side. When I wandered in there in my new clothes and with pockets bulging with money, Minette must have felt that all her prayers were answered. All she asked of life was a non-stop flow of booze, non-stop sex and non-stop excitement. Cabarets, restaurants, racetracks, gambling joints and bars were her natural habitat. She called money 'fun tickets' – in fact they were among the first words I ever heard her say. She had just finished a song (she couldn't really sing but when she was steaming and wriggling in front of a microphone nobody noticed), and she was heading for the bar. I'd tipped a waiter who'd brought some champagne to my table and she bent and handed me a twenty.

'You dropped some of your fun tickets, handsome,' she said.

'Keep it,' I said. I was drunk already. 'Have a drink. It might improve . . .'

She threw back her head and let go a throaty laugh that was more tuneful than her singing. She wasn't more than five foot two or three but her lean, whippy body was perfectly shaped and you didn't think of her as small. Her neck was slender and her head was sleek, with close-cropped dark hair and big, hooded violet eyes.

'Improve my singing, you were about to say.' She slung herself around a chair at the table and let me see her small breasts under the tight, silky material of her dress. 'I can think of three men who'd shoot you for saying that.'

I wasn't too drunk or too new to the city not to believe her. 'Well, I didn't mean . . . that is . . .'

'Happens I agree with you.' She pulled the champagne bottle from the bucket, put it to her mouth and drank in long, gurgling sucks. When she took it away the bottle was half empty and its top was red from her painted lips. 'If I c'd drink ten gallons of this stuff every day maybe I c'd sing like Bessie Smith.'

I suppose you could say that we tried to find out whether that was true. They threw us out of the Reveille sometime around dawn and we went back to my apartment and began a binge that lasted . . . well, to tell the absolute truth, I'm not sure how long it lasted. Looking back, it seems that sex was the only exercise I got and liquor the only nourishment, but that wasn't really true. We ate at fancy restaurants and in the big homes of the politcal bosses on the North Side. Minette had entrée into those circles and we went to many a lunch along Lake Shore Drive and many a soirée on Kenilworth Avenue. Me in a three piece silk suit with spats and a cane and Minette in a backless dress that ended at her knees, we'd arrive in the Studebaker and leave in a taxi because we were too plastered to travel any other way. There were lots of other bright young couples just like us – no one gave it a thought.

Minette also liked slumming. We'd drink rotgut rye in neighbourhood bars beside the El and listen to jazz in the negro joints that were slowing creeping south from the inner city ghetto. We ate spaghetti and drank dago red in places along Halstead Street in Little Italy where every second shop was a still or a fermentery. All that was risky, but the most dangerous thing of all, and the kind of fun that Minette liked most, was to hang around the cabarets and nightclubs frequented by the gangsters. The Reveille was one as I've said and also the Rendezvous and the Green Mill.

'C'mon, Dicky,' Minette would say, 'fill a pouch with fun tickets and let's go to the Mill.'

I'd deposited my funds in the First National Bank but after that deposit all transactions had been withdrawals. I kept a shoebox of the stuff in the apartment and simply filled a wallet or a couple of pockets before going out. Twenty thousand dollars stretched a long way in Chicago in those days – you could have a night on the town and come home with change out of fifty – if you didn't gamble, that is. Minette and I were gambling fools; fortunately she won at least as much as I lost so it wasn't so bad. Still, there weren't many sub-fifty buck nights.

One night I'll never forget, we togged up and were ready to go when I found the shoe box was unexpectedly empty. I laughed it off and borrowed a hundred from Minette but she had a funny look in her eye. She was wearing nothing but her shoes and stockings and a little dress that seemed to be made out of bits of glittering string.

'I know it's Spring,' I said, 'but won't you be cold?'

'Stupid. I'm gonna wear the coat.'

'Coat?'

'Honest, Dicky, you're so stewed so much of the time. Don't you remember bringing home the mink?'

I didn't. She went to the closet and pulled out a blue mink that shimmered in her hands. She slipped it on and her small body with its neat, trim head looked so alluring wrapped in the luxurious coat that I started to forget about going out. She pushed me away.

'Later, Daddy. We can do it on the coat if you like.'

In the car I wondered whether I'd emptied the shoebox to buy the coat. I couldn't remember. I told myself I was drinking too much and that it was time to slow down. But at the Green Mill, where we went that night, slowing down wasn't in style and all Minette understood was stepping on the gas. Result was that I was pretty high after an hour or two when a middle-sized man in a dark suit appeared in front of me out of the smoke haze.

'I'm Jack McGurn,' he said. 'Could we have a word?'

'Sure.' I dropped into a chair at my table. Minette was dancing with a pansy actor so there was nothing to worry about there. Some nights I had to practically peel the men off her and it was only my size and fit-looking appearance that let me get away with it. 'Sit down and have a drink.'

'I don't drink much.' McGurn sat down and watched me while I lit a cigar. 'I've got a nickname, you mighta heard it.'

'Teetotal Jack McGurn?' I laughed. It was incautious of me; he looked tough but he wasn't big and he was so smooth he seemed almost friendly.

'No, and I wouldn't joke about it if I was you,' he said softly.

I had enough liquor inside me not to notice the steadiness of his dark eyes and the ruthless set of his wide mouth. 'What can I do for you, Mr McGurn. Kelly's my name, by the way, Richard Kelly.'

'So they tell me. You could start by telling me where you got the coat.'

'Coat?' I felt that I'd said the word like that once before.

'Yeah, the mink. Looks exactly like one that got stolen from my car some time back. And here it turns up on your broad. This needs an explanation.'

'You don't think I stole it?'

'Tell you the truth, I don't know what a coat stealer looks like. But, no, I don't reckon you'da stole it. Point is, what you going to do about it.'

I laughed. 'I suppose you expect me to give it back?'

'It's an idea. What'd the broad say about that?'

'You'd hear it, so would everyone within three blocks.'

He laughed. 'Like that, eh? I got one just the same, maybe two. But what I mean is, who didja buy it from? I can't have punks stealing from my car and getting away with it.'

'I can't remember.' He suddenly seemed less friendly; the cigar tasted like ashes and I felt the need of a drink. 'Minny asked me the same question and I can't recall a thing about buying it. Apparently I was drunk when I brought it home. Sorry.'

'Sorry?' McGurn murmured. 'Sorry isn't the word.'

'Look, man to man, I just don't remember. You're an Irishman. You know how it is with us when we take on a drop too much. Kelly's the name, we're famous for forgettin'. . .'

The look that came over McGurn's face was enough to make you close your eyes and mouth and pray to still be alive when you opened them. Then he smiled; the smile spread across his lean, dark face and became a throaty laugh. The people around had fallen quiet while McGurn was talking, now the conversation started to buzz a little and bottles clinked against glasses. McGurn roared like a bear as his laughter shook him and everyone around laughed with him. I laughed too, with relief and in deep puzzlement.

Eventually, McGurn recovered. He got up from the table and walked towards the door shaking his head and gesturing for his pals to join him. Together they shouldered their way out of the place. I heard McGurn say 'Irish' and laugh again before he went through the door.

I smiled foolishly and had another drink. *Crisis over, Browning says the right thing again*, I thought. *Wonder what I said.* Minette appeared beside me; she was trembling slightly and I thought she must be cold in the string dress even though the temperature in the cabaret must have been in the eighties.

'What'sa matter, love?' I said.

'What did he want?'

'Wanted your mink. Said it was his.'

'Jesus. Did you give him the ticket?'

We'd checked the coat in on our arrival and I had the stub in my pocket. ''Course not. Simple mistake. Chap was a real gentleman and we settled it, one Irishman to another.'

'When he started laughing I thought you were dead, and me and everyone else . . . what did you *say!*'

''Bout what?'

'About Irishman.'

'Name's McGurn. Irish name like mine, ah . . .' Just then to be honest I couldn't recall what name I was using but I was sure I was on the right track.

'You fool. That was Machine Gun Jack McGurn.'

'What I said . . . McGurn . . .'

'He's about as Irish as Mussolini. His real name's Vincenzo De Mora.[23] He's Scarface Al Capone's chief enforcer.'

It was partly the heat and the smoke of course, but I fainted dead away.

CHAPTER EIGHTEEN

You might not think that a healthy young man who'd seen a bit of life could fritter away two years and twenty thousand dollars on nothing but drinking, womanising and raising hell. What an opportunity, you might say, to study or invest and make something of himself. Well, I let the opportunity slip by and did the hell-raising. As the fun tickets ran low Minette Kirby got nervous and one day she took a powder with her mink coat and the other trinkets I'd bought her. I moved from the Blackstone, of course and slowly descended through cheaper apartments to a series of rooms on the lower south side, getting ever closer to the El. The standard of the female company dropped too; I seem to recall an Ellen who wanted to marry me and a Susan who didn't, but the memories are dim.

Still, living was cheap and for a while I had debts to call in from my days of affluence, when I'd handed the stuff around like How-to-Vote cards. When the goodwill ran out I made ends meet by hock-ing things and then by betting on horses at which I've always been luckier than at cards, dice or women. But the horses will get you in the end and sometime during my third winter in Chicago I started to drive empty trucks to the Canadian border and bring them back full. I knew it was a mug's game but I'd lost my ambition. I was only twenty-seven[24] and, after the things I'd been through, I some-how felt that I was lucky to be alive and let it go at that.

I spent some of my time in the dago joints and rot-gut speakeas-ies, not slumming as before, but settling into them as comfortable haunts. I had my best times in the Spitfire Bar and Grill on South Clark Street when Bluey Tait, the Australian pilot who'd flown the Buffalo buyer in for the Yukon gold, was in town. Bluey would fly anybody and anything anywhere – liquor of course, small quality loads; Chinamen with suitcases full of marijuana from Mexico to California; flowers from the South to society weddings in the North; wives to lovers and jewellery to fences. On our first meeting in the Spitfire he looked closely at me and saw my hand shake as I lifted my drink.

'Are you hung?'

I nodded. It was three in the afternoon and I'd been up all night drinking and losing at cards. I'd had but one hour's sleep because my head hurt too much to let me sleep.

'I've got the cure, mate.'

'Listen, Blue, I'm very glad to see you, or I will be as soon as I feel human again. But don't come any of that goanna oil, dingo piss bullshit with me. I'm from the same neck of the woods, remember?'

'Nothing like that.' Blue shrugged his narrow shoulders into his flying jacket. He drained his beer and pulled his goggles out of a pocket. 'Come with me. Just as you are. Don't take another pill. You might bring along a little hair of the dog – not for now, for after.'

I bought a pint of rye and followed him out of the bar. My yellow Studebaker was history but Blue had a serviceable Ford in which he drove me to the airfield. I protested at every bump and had to hold my head steady in my hands but I managed to keep the seal on the rye, out of curiosity mainly. He used the Ford to tow a small plane out of a hangar – the airfield had undergone some improvements in the past two years and now had a tarred strip, several hangars and windsocks. For all its bright red and yellow paint and shiny metal, the plane looked fragile standing in the flat, open expanse with a pale grey sky above.

'I'm not going anywhere in that bloody thing,' I said.

'Just up and down, mate. A few minutes in the air's all you'll need. Think how nice it'll be to take a drink and light up a smoke with your head as clear as a bell.'

My head was pounding and my vision was blurred. My love of life itself must have been at a low ebb. I shrugged. Blue pulled a leather coat and helmet and some goggles from the plane and I put them on. The helmet was tight, but what the hell, a little more pain wasn't going to matter. Blue was bounding around like a cocker spaniel which was infectious. *Any minute now*, I thought, *he's going to ask me if I'm game.*

'You game, Dick?'

'I'm game.'

I climbed into the plane and Blue strapped me tight. The propeller noise seemed to pluck each hair on my head out with immense pain accompanying each pluck. Then cold air started rushing at me and I felt as if I was losing interest in my head altogether. My head was a lost cause – it was chest and legs that counted. The noise changed note and I opened my eyes to find myself up in the sky; forget about head and chest, my legs danced and trembled as if they had a life of their own. I screamed but the wind whipped the sound away. I sobbed and that made hardly any sound at all.

I think I went through all the horrors not gone through by the people who say their first flight didn't trouble them. I was their stand-in. I vomited over the side and wet myself. If I'd eaten anything in the past twenty-four hours I would've shat myself as well. I shook and pleaded with Blue to go down but he ignored me. He bellowed songs like 'John Brown's Body' and whooped as he threw the plane through some twists and loops. I almost broke fingers and wrists hanging on and my teeth chattered so hard I thought they would disintegrate.

The ground below changed colour from green to brown and yellow as Blue swooped about the sky. He roared over a hill missing it by six inches and went up into a cloud so that all sight and sound stopped for what seemed like an hour. Despite the cold I was dripping sweat and I could feel the expression of terror on my face setting into a concrete-like permanency. I'd given up pleading; I sat with my eyes open and waited to die in a blurr of cold liquid sound.

Then Blue cut back on the motor and we seemed to slide noiselessly through the air.

'Great, huh?' He sounded calm and relaxed behind me.

'Aah . . .' I said.

'How's the head?'

Fear had distracted me from the pain. I took a deep breath of the thin, cold air and let it out slowly. 'It's gone! My head's clear!'

'Told you. Greatest cure in the world. Take the stick.'

'What? Christ, no, Blue, don't!' I could feel the plane sliding away under my feet.

'You can drive, can't you, and ride a horse?'

'Yes! Yes! Shit, what's happening?'

'This is sort of a combination of the two – hands and feet. Grab the stick and touch the rudder . . .'

In the next hour Blue taught me to fly. He was a superb teacher and I forgot my fear in the thrill of mastering the skill. Blue was right, it *was* something like riding and driving and I was topnotch at both. Throw in first class vision and quick reflexes and you've got a pilot. The only thing I lacked was the iron nerve but, of course, with Blue there at the other controls, I didn't need it.

'You were terrific, mate,' he said after he landed. 'Best first timer I ever saw.'

'When can we do it again?'

'You're hooked.'

I was, too. I'd fly any time in any weather. I flew bi-planes and single-wingers, French, British jobs – whatever Blue was flying or whatever I could beg or borrow. I stayed sober in order to fly and dried out for days before presenting for my pilot's licence. In order to do that I needed an identity and it took a fair bit of work before

I was able to construct one. I got an affidavit from Blue to the effect that I was his compatriot, Richard Kelly, a fellow pilot who had lost all his personal possessions in an air accident. I got a driver's licence and had my much depleted bank account as further documentation.

I passed the test – I was going to say with flying colours, but even all my years in Hollywood wouldn't make me put down something as bad as that. As soon as I switched off, the examiner reached back and shook my hand.

'Thank you, Mr Kelly. It's sure been a pleasure flying with you, and Francis J. Watts don't say that to many.'

'Thank you, Mr Watts.'

'Francis. Anybody flies like you do calls me Francis.'

Over the next year and a bit I went into business with Bluey Tait. We must have crossed the continental United States a hundred times, from Montana to Texas, California to the east coast, and even to Cuba a couple of times, for booze and cigars. Chicago was our base: it was central, navigation was easy, to and from, with the lakes as markers, and it was comforting to see all that flat land around. Another plus was the administration of the city: this was fixed in almost every possible way and the officials must have got neckache looking the other way considering some of the cargoes we flew in.

I never made it back to the Blackstone, but I lived pretty well again, although hiring and maintaining aircraft and insurance costs were high in those days. The only cheap part of the operation was the fuel which sold for about twenty cents per gallon. When the freight business was slow, Blue and I gave lessons but I never went up with novices. We also did a bit of passenger work, flying big De Havilands for people in a hurry. I enjoyed it all but in particular the young woman we hired to handle things in our little hole-in-the-wall office on Division Street near Tower Town, which was named after the big Chicago water tower and was the city's nearest thing to Greenwich Village.

Terri Driver was twenty years old; she'd graduated *magna cum laude* from some secretarial college in the east and she could answer the phone, take dictation, calculate costs and make coffee all at the same time. She was the first person to answer 'Aussie Air's' advertisement in the *Tribune*, and we later found out that she'd camped outside the office for two hours before Blue arrived to interview applicants. I was Aussie Air's late-arriving junior partner. Times were already tough in the mid-twenties and Terri was glad of the job and the ten bucks we paid her most weeks. Despite the efficient way she kept the books, funds sometimes ran low and major repair bills or a job falling through at the last minute could practically clean us out. Terri juggled things, went without, got us credit when it seemed impossible and held the operation together. We told her to pay herself a bonus when we were flush but I doubt she ever did. I was in love with her of course, but I never got to first base.

'You think I haven't met your type, just because you're an Aussie?' she said to me in the office one day. The office was a likely grappling place because there was hardly room for two people to stand without touching bodies at some point. Terri was of medium height; she had frizzy blond hair which frequently had a pencil tucked in it, sometimes a cigarette. She had big, round breasts that any normal man would want to touch. They were only inches from me now.

'Don't know what you mean,' I said, inching one hand forward towards her waist. 'I'm not a type, I'm unique, I . . .'

'Hah! Unique, you ain't. You're great fun, Dick Kelly, or whatever your name is, but you know what I see every time I look into your big brown eyes?'

'No, what?' Another inch and I could slide my hand around her back.

'Packed suitcases. You're always packed and ready to go. As I say, I've seen the type from Maine to Montana.' She stepped sideways and plunged into a pile of papers. I was hot for her and didn't want to give up without a struggle. I crowded close again and touched her hair.

'Quit it!'

'What did you mean about . . . whatever my name is? That a crack?'

Terri was a smart girl. She could see I was getting sore and she knew what do about it, like a boxer who knows how to put a combination together. Jab – she leaned towards me and gave me a light kiss on the lips. Body punch – 'Your name is Brown, or something like that.' Right cross – 'And you're afraid to fly alone. Want me to read your character some more?'

I slumped down into the only chair in the office and lit a cigarette. 'That's enough, Terri. How did you know about the name?'

'A guy walked in here one day . . . don't worry, he doesn't live in Chicago, he was just passing through, and he said he'd seen you come in here and he thought he knew you from Australia. An Aussie, like me, he asks. When I said that was right, he muttered Brown, Brown something like that. Said his name was MacKnight. Dick, you've gone pale!'

I was shaking. My deserted wife, Elizabeth MacKnight, had cousins and family connections all over the place. As far as I knew I was still married to her and the last thing I wanted was for her to get wind of my whereabouts. She was quite capable of crossing the world to haul me back and if she was still of the same mind as she had been six or seven years before she would blackmail me into compliance.[25] But Terri had said he was just passing through . . . I could shave off my moustache . . . maybe we could shift our base further east or west . . . my mind raced, then I recalled the other thing she'd said.

'Are you all right, Dick. Want some water or something?'

'No, no. Er . . . Terri, what was that about flying alone?'

'You never do it. I've seen you wriggle and twist to get out of it. You'll fly anything with wings but not on your own.'

'Don't tell Blue, for God's sake!'

She laughed. 'He knows. He jokes about it.'

'Jokes?'

'Said he was going to enter you in a solo round America race.'

'Jesus!'

'Don't worry about it.' She pulled the pencil from her hair and started ticking off items on a sheet. 'You've other things to worry about. Times is bad, Dick. Aussie Air ain't doin' so good.'

When she joked like that you knew she was serious. 'How close to the edge are we?'

'Off the edge and fallin' fast, if you'll excuse the language.'

I lit her a cigarette from the stub of mine and we both blew smoke and contemplated the future. At that moment Blue dashed into the office. He was wearing a greasy overall, had oil and muck on his hands and face and the only clean thing about him was the slip of paper he held in his hand.

'Hally-bloody-loolyah!' he yelled.

'What, what?' I said.

'You'll never bloody believe it. The other day I got talking out at the airfield to this bloke. Long, tall streak he was, Texan. Said he was a rich millionaire, well, they all do, don't they? Anyway, he said he was making a flying picture in Hollywood and needed pilots and planes.'

'Hollywood,' Terri said. 'Oh, yeah.'

'No, listen. I told him Dick 'n' me could fly any fucking thing . . . excuse me, Terri, and we could get him planes. All it took was money.'

'That's right,' Terri said.

'So, he turns up again today and hands me a cheque – twenty-five fucking thousand dollars!'

Terri shook her head. 'Has to be a dud.'

'Not this guy,' Blue said. 'I reckon he's genuine.'

I felt excitement and a surge of hope. Hollywood again, away from Chicago and some sneaking, tale-telling MacKnight. 'What's his name, Blue?'

'I dunno. I can't read the signature. Hughie . . . Howie.'

'Let me see that!' Terri snatched the cheque and held it to the light. 'Christ,' she said, 'Howard Hughes.'

CHAPTER NINETEEN

Blue and I spent the next six months acquiring aircraft and flying them to California. We got a Spad, an SE-5, Sopwith Pups and Camels, Fokkers – relics from the war. Hughes had scouts in Europe doing the same thing and he hired war aces like Roscoe Turner and stunt flyers like Paul Mantz[26] to throw them around the skies.

Blue laid claim to a dozen 'kills' in the war so he was clearly an ace; I was never quite sure what I was. Certainly not an ace and no stunt flyer either. It didn't bother me at first; I just flew the planes, always with a co-pilot, to Mines Field in Inglewood (the site of that modern monster, the LA International Airport – Jesus, the scares and disappointments I've had there).

Some of the planes we bought outright with Hughes' money, others we leased, and some we bought ourselves and leased to Hughes. We were paid salaries, commissions and we were to get special bonuses and allowances for flying for the cameras. It was all very complicated and it soon became obvious that Blue and I needed Terri to keep things straight. Besides, I was still hoping to get under her guard somehow and show her what a good time we could have together. I admitted as much the day we arrived in Los Angeles as a team. A cool December day it was; we had flown in, of course, in a Fokker, and Terri had telephoned ahead for rooms in a medium grade hotel in downtown LA. At the hotel I waited until Blue was out of earshot and then I herded Terri into a corner.

'Blue's buggered,' I said. 'He'll sleep like the dead. D'you know that this place has giant bath tubs and giant beds. It'd be crazy for us to get lonely. You know how I feel about you.'

'You want to wash my back and sleep with me?'

'Yes.'

'Willing to do something for me?'

'Anything.'

'You know I can't fly?'

'Ummm.'

'I want you to teach me. Take me up tomorrow for my first lesson. I've never even touched the controls. I'm a flying virgin. What d'you say, Dick?'

'Don't drown in the bath,' I said. *Nothing* was going to get me up in the air without another fully qualified pilot – *nothing*! I was very careful about the assignments I accepted; I never flew a French Spad for example, terrific planes though they were, because they were one-seaters.

So things stayed as they were. We rented a house in Inglewood with a cottage at the back where Terri slept in something approaching respectability. After a week or so Blue moved the first of a long series of girlfriends into the house and I found myself odd man out. I spent a lot of innocent time with Terri, playing cards and such, and some sinning time in the bars and whorehouses. Hughes kept us pretty busy working on the planes, submitting chalkboard plans of battle scenes and scouting for locations all over the western United States. He wanted fluffy clouds, or he wanted fields below, or a river or a mountain. He wanted everything and he wanted it yesterday.

Strange as it may sound, I worked for Howard Hughes for nearly seven months before I laid eyes on him. Blue didn't see him again after their initial meetings. We got memos and phone calls and followed orders. Terri submitted invoices and cheques got cashed. A few days before filming began I started to get an eerie feeling that

I was working for a ghost. I couldn't shake the feeling off and it undermined my confidence.

'Does he exist?' I asked Terri one day.

'Search me. His cheques are good. Isn't there someone you can ask? You seem to know your way around this town a bit.'

I did, of course, from my sojourn five years before. The place had grown a lot, spread in all directions. There were more people and many more cars. Bare hillsides now had white stucco bungalows on them and the vacant lots that had been a feature of the streets and even some of the shopping districts had filled up. I'd kept what would now be called a low profile; I had debts and disgraces from my earlier days in Hollywood that I preferred to forget. I also had enemies – Douglas Fairbanks for one, a certain bootlegger, the IWW – quite enough to make me feel happiest with my goggles on and my silk scarf obscuring part of my handsome face.

But this was serious. I knew Hollywood and knew how big the lies there could be, how a scheme could collapse overnight no matter how huge and solid it might seem by daylight. Blue and I owed money on the planes and needed the salaries and commissions to keep coming for quite some time if we were going to come out of *Hell's Angels*, which was the name of the picture, in the black. I cast around for someone to confide in, someone who wouldn't betray me if it was in his best interest not to. Someone unprincipled, conniving and ruthless. The answer was obvious – H. Eliot Silkstein, my former agent.

I drove Aussie Air's Dodge convertible north along Western Avenue the fifteen miles or so to Sunset Boulevard where Silkstein had his office. The pink pile of the Beverly Hills Hilton still dominated the straight stretch where the deals were done and the reputations were made and destroyed. I hadn't telephoned because the explanations were too complicated: how did you tell someone you'd run out on that you were back, using a different name and either about to be rich or about to be bankrupt? It wasn't something to do on the phone, maybe it wasn't something to do at all.

I parked in the street between a yellow De Soto and a black Hispano Suiza that looked like the twin of the one Pedro Cortez and I had escaped from Mexico in. We'd sold it for a song just over the border so maybe it was. *If the owners of these cars are clients of Silkstein's*, I thought, *then the old crook must be doing all right.* I put my hand on the plate glass door and glanced automatically at the list of Silkstein's companies – his vanity had him display them right out on the street. The list was longer than ever but there was a change in the layout. Where 'H. Eliot Silkstein' had appeared in one inch high letters over the list of companies, now 'N. Robert Silkstein' was written instead, in two inch high letters.

I'd never heard that H. Eliot had any sons but, given that screwing women was his favourite recreation, it seemed more than likely. And Hollywood being Hollywood, the sons were often bigger rogues than the fathers – think of Selznick – so anything I could have tried with Dad, I reasoned, might work with Junior. I noticed the updated decor in the passageway and on the stairs where I'd first encountered John Gilbert and his squeaky voice. Updated but not improved; it was showier and more vulgar if anything, vaguely Viking in mood. That was a good sign. Not such a good sign was the woman at the reception desk – same tight blond curls, same tight red mouth, same Miss Dupre.

I was wearing a modified version of my flying outfit – new leather jacket, silk scarf, well-pressed corduroys, with the raffish moustache and slightly curling hair, and she didn't recognise me. The last time she'd have seen me I'd have been in a Palm Beach suit with my hair lacquered into place.

'Yes?' She had a way of making the word sound like 'Screw off, buddy.'

'Commander Kelly to see Mr Silkstein.'

She consulted the book on her desk but didn't really need to. 'Appointment?' she said, not looking up.

'Afraid not.'

'Afraid you can't see him then. And please, don't smoke in here. It affects my sinuses.'

I'd taken a cigarette from my silver case. 'H. Eliot's cigars didn't bother you.'

'I beg your pardon.'

'The first time I saw you you were on guard out here while the boss screwed a redhead. I guess he must've been doing some work at home if he's got this son, Robert N.'

'N. Robert. Who are you?'

I lit the cigarette, blew the smoke away and leaned over the desk to whisper. 'Dick Browning. Remember the card – "Beverly Hills" Browning? You'd have got a laugh out of that along with everyone else.'

She straightened up and patted her hair. 'There were criminal charges, if I'm not mistaken. I'm sorry, but Mr Silkstein isn't seeing any out-of-work actors today.'

I'd taken the precaution of bringing along a substantial cheque signed by Hughes and not yet cashed as well as a leasing arrangement also signed by him as principal of his film company. I put the documents on top of the open appointments book. 'I'm not an out-of-work actor, Miss Dupre, I'm an in-work actor and I work for Howard Hughes.'

She gaped; I picked up the cheque and blew on it. Miss Dupre buzzed the boss.

'Better be big, I'm busy.'

'There's a Mr Browning here, Mr Silkstein, he . . .'

'Kelly,' I hissed.

'A Mr Kelly, he . . .'

'Commander.'

'Commander Kelly was a client of your father's, he . . .'

'Handout?'

'No. He works for Howard Hughes.'

'Send him in.'

I retrieved my papers and went through the door that had 'N. Robert Silkstein' on it in three inch high letters without knocking. In this room much had changed; the elaborate, heavy furniture had given way to sleeker stuff and the same was true of the inhabitants. N. Robert was as neat and whippy as H. Eliot had been slobby and gross. *The old man must have crossbred with something racy*, I thought as I walked over to the desk. The man standing behind it was on the short side but he made that seem like a virtue. His light grey suit was perfect, so was his shirt and tie, haircut and everything else in sight.

'Commodore Kelly,' he said. 'Siddown.'

The shock of the voice helped to drop me into a chair. I'd expected something very east coast, not lower East Side, New York. He came around the desk and shook my hand.

'Whatsa matter? Oh yeah, the voice. My old man sent me to New York for my education. I speak better Eyetalian than I do . . .'

He was going to say Yiddish but thought better of it. I put his age at about twenty-five, but it was the time of Irving Thalberg remember, and there was no reason to think that this kid might not be a solid chip off the old block. 'I knew your father,' I said. 'I worked with Fairbanks on . . .'

'*Robin Hood*,' he said. 'Is that you? I remember now. The old man usta talk about the limey who got in Dutch with some bootlegger . . .'

'"Tidal Eddy",' I said. 'I hope he's not still around.'

'Naw. He floated onta Santa Monica beach one morning and he wasn't swimming on accounta the bullet in his head. What can I do for you? Did the old man owe you dough? If so, forget it. I ruled the line a year ago.'

'No, nothing like that. I want information and advice.' I told him about my arrangements with Hughes and asked for his estimation of the prospects for the picture and the likelihood of Hughes paying in full. He lit a big, black cigar as I spoke and he seemed to be enjoying my story more with each puff. I felt like throwing in a few jokes – I'd never known a speech of mine to go off so well. 'I'm not even sure that Hughes exists.'

'Hughes is a sucker,' he said, 'and a rich sucker at that. You'll get your dough. But if you play your cards right you'll make twice as much as you're counting on now.'

'How?'

He leaned across the desk. His dark eyes glittered in his pale, thin face. 'With the right agent you can clean up – fees for stunts, danger money, expenses, insurance, lawsuits . . .'

'Lawsuits?' I was alarmed; the last thing I wanted was an appearance in a court of law. I imagined the US had extradition arrangements with Canada. And what if a MacKnight saw my photo in a paper? Silkstein noted my reaction and probably read it accurately. He waved his cigar.

'Threatened lawsuits. Leave it all to me.'

'Your father took ten per cent.'

'Some things don't change . . . Dick.'

I wouldn't say it was a comfortable feeling, being a client of the Silkstein Agency again, but at least some of my fears had been put at rest. If N. Robert was the publicist his father had been, it might be possible for me to emerge from under my goggles and try my hand at acting again. Something about the life still appealed to me although it had turned so sour the first time. I drove back to Inglewood to find Blue and his current woman standing in front of the house. Blue was smoking which was unusual for him and looking very agitated.

'What's going on?'

Terri appeared at the door, her hair bristling with pencils. 'Hello, Dick,' she said. 'I need to bank that cheque today – better safe than sorry.'

'I've endorsed it. Could someone please tell me what's happening. Are we being evicted?'

'No, old sport,' Blue said. 'We're on. Sudden development. Scramble, like in the war.'

'Shit. Why?'

'God knows. Don't grizzle. You're going to get your wish.'

'What d'you mean?'

'Hughes is going to be there and he's going to fly one of the kites himself.'

CHAPTER TWENTY

The scene at Mines Field was a madhouse. There were planes lined up in ranks and others sitting around as if everybody had forgotten about them. Men were wandering around with schedules and take-off times and sketches of manoeuvres to be performed in the air. There was a lot of shouting, wind-checking, fuel pumping and wiping with oily rags. Blue left his girl in the car with a flask of gin and a lapful of magazines and marched across towards the centre of the action.

'Hey, what're you doing?' I said.

'Getting up front. Maybe I can be the first plane in the air.'

'If Hughes is really here you'll be second at best,' I said. 'Mark my words.'

'That'll do. Come on.'

'Think I'll have a look at the kites.'

I hung back and let Blue go. Truth to tell, I'd rather have been back in the car with the girl and the gin. I planned to do as little flying as possible. I'd seen some of those chalkboard sketches Roscoe Turner and the others laughed over and they made my blood run cold. I fancied myself piloting the plane with the camera, or one of the cameras – well back and hold 'er steady, that'd be the ticket.

A cheer went up and a tall, dark man strode from the clutch of people towards a Morse scout plane parked a few hundred feet away. This was Hughes all right. He wore a flying jacket, white shirt with no tie, baggy cotton pants and white tennis shoes. He shambled a bit, looked shy and I thought that he'd have to put his knees under his chin to get those legs into the cockpit. I'd never flown a Morse and neither, I found out later, had Hughes. The plane had a rotary engine which might have made a difference to the handling. Hughes waved and there was another cheer as the Morse took off.

Up into the blue Californian sky she soared and at about four hundred feet Hughes banked sharply left: the plane flipped and went into a flat spin. People were screaming and running around. Someone with presence of mind yelled for a fire truck and of course there wasn't one. I stared as the Morse crashed to earth. I started running before she hit and was one of the first on the spot. You'll hear that Hughes walked away brushing bits of the fabric from his hair but it wasn't like that at all. We had to lever struts and cut wires to get to him and he was out cold when we pulled him free. He was so tall it seemed to take an age to extract him. His face was covered with blood and I thought he was dead.

There was no more flying that day. Everybody hung around glumly and the excited up-and-running atmosphere was gone like a puff of smoke. I did manage to get in a word with one of the assistant directors (there was a team of them) about flying one of the camera planes. He'd seen me do my bit at the crash site and he nodded and made a note. At the time I thought it was a waste of breath; with Hughes dead the movie would probably fold but you can never do too much protecting of your own ass, that's Browning's motto.

Hughes didn't die, of course; he had a depressed fracture of the cheekbone and some other injuries but he was back on the set within a couple of weeks. If you haven't seen the movie – and why would you? it creaks like a barn door these days – it's basically the story of some World War I pilots getting their fighting lives and love lives entangled. James Hall played the pure-heart, with a cowardly brother played by Ben Lyon. Between these two came Jean Harlow, who was pure-heart's fiancée until she got into bed with Bad Ben for a reason I could never fathom. The movie was originally shot as a silent with some Swede[27] in the Harlow role. She wouldn't do when they decided to change the thing into a talkie so they got a new script and a new girl. But that was all after we'd done our daredevil deeds in the sky.

Harry Perry was the chief cameraman and he knew his business. What he didn't know about flying he learned, partly from Blue. When he knew enough to handle a plane I went up with him and, as I knew a bit about filming, we got along fine. I spent most of my time in the camera plane or flying an observation kite high above the action. I had to move quickly to avoid James Whale, who actually did a lot of the direction, because he wanted me to pilot the observation plane with him as passenger and he couldn't fly.

Going up with Hughes, which I did several times, was a different matter. He could fly with the best of them (the Morse he crashed must have had a mechanical fault), so I wasn't worried on that score, but he was crazy. They say he grew his hair and fingernails and slept in his own shit later and I fully believe it. He was a nice-looking guy, even with the battered cheek, but he didn't seem to know it. He wore tennis shoes most of the time, even with a suit, and on him it looked all right. All the women seemed to think so and it wasn't just his money that attracted them. You had to listen very closely to catch what he said because he mumbled in a thick southern accent. Now, in those days you had yell to make yourself heard in a plane.

'Muh muh muh, muh,' Hughes would say.

'What, Mr Hughes?' I'd yell.

'Muh, muh . . .'

'What?'

'Bank right, you son of a bitch!' he'd scream. 'I can't see a goddamn thing!'

Sometimes he'd want to get close to the action – I mean screaming dogfights between the Fokkers and the Sopwith Pups, with planes buzzing around like a swarm of wasps – and I'd have to think quickly to forestall him.

'Get in close, goddammit! Closer!'

'Can't. We'll be in shot.'

That held him back once or twice but he was a crazy bastard as I say, and he took it into his head to get me to make one of his close passes, no matter what the cost. I knew it was coming and I knew he'd fire me if he didn't get his own way, so I had one of the mechanics rig up a switch under the control panel of the Avro Avian we were using as an observation plane. By flipping the switch I could fake engine trouble and get the hell out of a tight spot. I told the mechanic the switch was part of a stunt.

Operations had moved ten miles west of Hollywood to the San Fernando Valley where there was more space and even clearer sky. Aussie Air had moved to a house in Encino. It was a very comfortable house but small, which didn't matter so much as Blue seemed to have given up the girls. This puzzled me but he was working so hard, doing so much flying and maintenance work, that I thought he'd temporarily taken a break from the broads to aid his concentration. He was drinking much less too. Silkstein had done his job and secured us a favourable contract that screwed every possible penny out of Hughes' production company.

All in all, it would have been a peaceful and profitable time if not for two irritants: one was my continual failure to make any time with Terri; I seemed to be losing even more ground there. Two was this bee in Hughes' bonnet to get me to fly wingtip-to-wingtip with some fighter spraying bullets.

I tried to duck Hughes, to go up with the cameras or to bury myself up to my ass in the workings of a plane; sometimes, I pulled my goggles down, set my cap squarely on my head and pretended not to hear when Kelly was being paged. But eventually he caught me. Or rather, one of his assistants did – Mr Hughes didn't do much stomping around in the dust. This kid, dressed up like a polo player in jodhpurs and boots (God knows why, people did that sort of thing in Hollywood), sat down next to me in the canteen.

'C'n I have your autograph?'

I was off guard. I had a good slug of brandy in my coffee and was feeling pretty relaxed. 'Sure, kid.' I scrawled 'Dick Kelly – RAF' on the slip of paper he'd put down.

The kid looked at it. 'Thank you, Mr Kelly. Mr Hughes wants you to be ready to fly with him in ten minutes. If you'd like to finish your coffee and come with me?'

There was nothing to do but drink up and follow him. The Avro Avian was painted a bright red with white crosses on the wings which didn't do me any good for a start – blood and bandages, if you see what I mean. As I walked towards it I encountered Blue, who was all togged up and ready to fly. Blue had been a bit cool with me of late I fancied, probably because he thought I had all the cushy jobs. Well, he was off mark today.

'Hello, Blue, old mate,' says I. 'What's on now?'

'Dogfight and nose dive,' Blue grunts.

He adjusted his helmet and moved away.

That's bad, I thought. *I'll bet this maniac wants me to follow the diver and pull out ten feet above the sod.*

Hughes was waiting by the plane, looking impatient.

'Muh, muh, muh,' he says.

'Sorry, Mr Hughes.' That was always the safest line to take with him.

We went up; it was a lovely clear day. The Santa Monica hills were to the west and I could see the Pacific, twenty miles or so to the south-west. None of this meant anything to Hughes. He grunted directions – altitudes and speeds – and stared down at the other planes as they zoomed up and began to arrange themselves around the sky. Blue was flying a Spad and it became clear from the dummy runs that he was the one to do the dive. I shuddered as I watched them banking and wheeling around, just missing each other, and making a terrible racket. The wind was snatching bits of sound – screaming engines, buzzing and whistling – and throwing them around like leaves in a high wind.

Eventually they got the patterns sorted out. Blue did the manoeuvre perfectly – roaring down to earth and pulling out at the last minute. Men on the ground were ready to prepare the fake explosion and there were at least three camera planes in close attendance.

'Too crowded to get close, Mr Hughes,' I yelled.

'They're doin' another dummy run, Mistuh Kelly. Ah want you to go down there all th' way.'

'Christ!' I yelled. 'Why?'

'Ah wah wah mum ah ah rah.'

'What?'

'Ah want to see if he gets th' expression on his face raht.'

That's how mad he was. Is it any wonder he spent most of the last years of his life watching movies in Las Vegas? Well, I had an ace in the hole so I wasn't too worried. The planes got into formation; thumbs went up and engines howled. A Fokker chased the Spad across the sky and Blue did some fancy banks and dips. I stayed as close to the action as I could without getting involved in the actual aerobatics.

'Hyah he goes,' Hughes yelled. 'Stay with th' son of a bitch!'

To show willing, I banked sharply and got into position to join the dive. I even revved up and let the nose dip. Then I flipped the switch.

Nothing happened.

I was so startled I kept on with what I'd been doing, going into the dive with the engine whining and the air rushing past us. By the time I came to my senses I was plummeting towards earth at a speed that threatened to tear the wings off. I tried to pull out of the dive but the switch chose that moment to come into action and the engine coughed and died. Out of the corner of my eye I saw the surprise on Blue's face as my dive matched his. Hughes was shouting something which I couldn't understand – probably telling Blue to look more frightened. He should've seen me: I was working the stick and trembling all over and my bowels were loosening. The San

Fernando Valley was rushing up to hit me in the face. I flipped the switch on and off; the engine came to life long enough to increase the speed of the dive and then cut out again. I was screaming, ready to babble my prayers. I thumbed the switch, felt my thumb dislocate and the engine caught. It all seemed to go into slow motion then; I had time to look across at Blue, see what he was doing and do the same. The Avro Avian shuddered, seemed to hang in the air, and then pulled out of the dive.

Blue's face, as we sailed up in tandem, was like a clown's when he takes an unexpected fall. I wiped sweat from my face with my right hand and found I was holding up my dislocated thumb. Blue grinned, gave me a thumbs up in reply and peeled off to join the formation. I was flying by memory and if Hughes spoke to me again while we were up I didn't hear him. I got the plane down somehow and switched off. Sweat had drenched me from my hair to my socks. I had a desperate need to feel firm ground beneath my feet but I couldn't move and I needed alcohol and tobacco as I'd never needed them before. Hughes took off his harness, raised himself up in the seat and swivelled round. He was holding out a long, bony hand that was as steady as a statue. I wiped my hand on my pants and shook with him; he had a strong grip and I felt my thumb slip back into place with the pressure. Maybe that stopped me from shaking, I don't know, but he didn't seem to notice anything amiss.

There was a muffled boom over to the east. Flames shot into the air and Blue's Spad zoomed through the smoke, climbing. Hughes nodded approvingly.

'Mistuh Kelly,' he said. 'You an' yore buddy sure can fly. It's been a privilege, suh, to go up with you. Thank you.'

'Thank *you*, Mr Hughes,' I said.

CHAPTER TWENTY ONE

In 1928 it seemed like everyone in Hollywood was working for Hughes. And not just in Hollywood; some time that year we shifted operations again, this time up to San Francisco because the Oakland area had the sort of clouds Hughes wanted. He wanted clouds like the ones over France in the war years. God knows why he thought there was anything special about them. I'd been under those clouds in 1917: when they were low it rained, when they were high the bombers could see where to drop their loads and could give accurate instructions to the artillery. Clouds were bad news either way. But we flew back and forth between the San Fernando Valley and Oakland, filming, carrying equipment and personnel, and all the time Aussie Air was coining money.

It was very different from my previous stint in Hollywood. Then I had plenty of time for lolling about swimming pools, drinking in speakeasies and sleeping late between silk sheets in congenial company. Now it was work, work, work. I was away from the Encino house for a week at a time and Blue and Terri were away a lot too. Blue taught Terri to fly which took up some time and she was at us constantly to get her work in the film. No dice. Hughes was mad but not *that* mad. People were flying crazy at the time, women included. It was a few years before Amelia Earhart really hit the headlines but she was already well known and cross-country air races featuring women pilots were popular novelty attractions.

If it had got out that a woman was working on *Hell's Angels*, every joystick-happy aviatrix in America would have headed for the spot.

So I was on my own a good deal in Oakland and Encino but often so tired that I didn't miss the fast life. I'm not saying I didn't hit the whorehouses and bars from time to time, I did, but I was wary of meeting up with Fairbanks and some of the others from the old days. I did some drinking with Ben Lyon, who liked to raise hell once in a while. He did some of his own flying in the film so we had that in common.

Looking back, there were plenty of good times but I remember Hollywood nightlife at the time as full of pitfalls and dangers. Like the night I went drinking with Lyon and his friend, Gary Cooper, at the Coconut Grove. Cooper, who was starting to go places in the silents, was good company, especially when he had a few drinks inside him. He seemed to attract lively people to him in those days. He certainly attracted Clara Bow (but then who didn't, if he had the right equipment and inclination which Coop did by all accounts). This night was in honour of someone's birthday, I forget who, maybe Mack Sennett. Carole Lombard was there without the 'e' on her name – she added that later, after she got beyond doing Sennett comedies. Some other people from the Sennett gang were in the party, including Billy Bevan.

Bevan wore a brush moustache on screen and looked entirely different without it. I was on guard the second he spoke.

'Gid'day,' he said, 'they tell me you're an Australian.'

'That's right.'

'So'm I. William Bevan Harris. Born in Orange, New South. How about you?'

'Ah, Sydney.'

'Don't seem too sure, mate.'

He was laying it on thickly. There were a few Australians in Hollywood but they all adopted American accents pretty quickly, or, like me, used a sort of modified English voice for reasons of status. I made the mistake of laying *that* on too thickly just then.

'Awfully good to meet you,' I said. 'I say, Ben . . .'

'What didya do in the war?'

'I beg your pardon.'

'Shirker, eh? Thought so.'

'You little pipsqueak. I'll . . .'

'Whoa, Billy!' This was Carole Lombard screaming as Bevan jumped into her lap pretending to be afraid of me. Of course I'm left there looking stupid and desperately in need of a funny line.

'I can see you're an Australian, Billy,' I said. 'You jump like a kangaroo.'

Well, you mightn't think much of it, but it drew a laugh and got me out of a tight spot. I was constantly on edge, you see, about being recognised as 'Beverly Hills' Browning, or William Hughes (the name I'd served and deserted under) or Tony Grace, the South African photographer. If you've carried the same name through all of your life, good luck to you – you don't know what security and peace of mind you've had.

Cooper had been watching me while this was going on and after my moment of awkwardness had passed he shook off the blonde who was trying to tear his arm from its socket and sat down next to me.

'You ever do any shootin', Dick?' he drawled. This was a long speech for Coop.

'Yes, I have. Why d'you ask, Coop?'

'Thought you might've. You got the eyes. Kinda steady. Shoot men?'

I'd recovered from the fright Bevan had given me and could assemble a plausible and half-true story in my mind. 'In the war, yeah. I was a sniper.'

'Too young for the war. How's it feel? To shoot men?'

We had a lot of liquor and a long talk on the subject. Because of the liquor I can't recall the talk, but I told Cooper about the stillness of mind and body you needed to shoot straight and the ways of talking yourself into the shot. He must have listened because, many years later, when I saw him in *Sergeant York,* I could see him putting my tips into his performance. I had some dealings with Cooper, not all of them pleasant, like when we were making *The Plainsman* for His Majesty de Mille, but that's another story.

After the crowd had thinned and I was looking around for someone to have a last drink with, a guy came mincing towards me. He swayed from the hips down as though he was dancing except there was no music playing.

'Can I buy you a drink?'

He was wearing a white, double-breasted suit and smelt of toilet water. Fifteen years later in Hollywood I spent a bit of time with Raymond Chandler who seemed to be fascinated by the faggots around town. I remember telling him about this one and remarking that the weight of his gold bracelet might have explained his limp wrist. Chandler laughed and said he could use that, I don't know whether he did. Point is, the Coconut Grove, like most of the nightspots, was no place for a presentable man without a female companion.

I brushed the guy off and drove home to Encino. On the way I made a mental list of the girls I could've taken with me that night. It was a pretty long list but I knew why I hadn't called any of them. I wanted Terri.

But Terri was away on business in Texas, trying to negotiate a deal whereby Aussie Air could supply aviation fuel to the aircraft in the film and maybe to the soon-to-be Los Angeles Airport that everybody was talking about. Blue was in Chicago winding up some unfinished business there.

I put myself to sleep with a bottle that night and for the next couple of nights. In the day I wandered around some of the studios vaguely thinking about more congenial movie work – the kind that involved lounging around in silk pyjamas and cuddling up with

Gloria Swanson. The Keystone lot was a madhouse, of course: they'd be filming three or four different stories at the one time inside, and outside, with the cars whizzing around and ladders collapsing – it was quite risky to walk around without a crash helmet. All the shooting sets were noisy, physical sorts of places compared to the smooth, purring sets of today. I saw a fight break out between some bit players on the set of *Dream of Love,* where Joan Crawford was in a clinch with someone, and they went on filming as if nothing had happened.

Moving around Hollywood, I kept an eye open for the cops and bootleggers and IWW men I'd run into previously, but I had no problems. It was such a changeable place – people got rich and poor overnight, fat and thin, moved away, came back and changed their names. This applied to all sorts of people – Gloria Swanson was Gloria Mae at one time, and the Europeans changed their names more often than they changed their suits. Madmen like Von Stroheim (for whom I did a day's work, all dolled up in knee britches and periwig, as an extra on *Queen Kelly,* before they took him off it) dropped in 'Vons' and extra handles as it suited them. People were not what they seemed.

It was about this time that I took up photography again. My good old Leica was in some locker in Vancouver as the confiscated property of the gunrunner, Richard Browning. I bought another Leica, an updated one with extra knobs and switches which I never learned to use properly. I took some shots of Hollywood's places of interest and I must dig them out and take a look at them. They're fifty years old, some of 'em – might be worth some money. [A bundle of photographs enclosed in an envelope on which 1928-9 is scrawled were found with the tapes. Browning's photography lacks distinction; he seems to have had difficulty with focus and in keeping his hand steady. Most of the pictures are of Hollywood watering holes like the Garden of Allah, the Beachcombers, the Cinebar etc. There are a few snapshots of prominent players, such as Marion Davies and Dolores Del Rio, but they have a hurried appearance as if Browning scarcely had time, let alone permission, to take the picture. One picture shows a tall man with light-coloured hair brushed back, wearing a leather flying jacket. He has his arm around a woman with curly fair hair. This may be a photograph of Blue Tait and Terri Driver but, unlike the other photographs, this one does not have Browning's scrawled identification on the back. Ed.]

In fact, I was filling in time as things went quiet on the movie and I waited to see how the business would develop. All that changed, however, when I got back to the house one night after a bit of a party at Alma Rubens' place on Hollywood Boulevard. I remember it clearly even though I was a bit stewed: it was dawn and the sun was just coming up over the trees. We had a nice garden with flowerbeds and a hammock strung between two trees. I thought of taking a nap in the hammock but I could see the sunlight glinting on a whole pile of empty bottles that lay in it and I didn't want to deal with bottles just then. I'd picked up the mail from the box out front and I sat down on the porch at back to look at it. I was hoping for a postcard from Terri in Texas.

Instead there were bills and a couple of sealed envelopes. One was from the *Hell's Angels* production office telling me that I should report to the Valley tomorrow for the shooting of an important scene, something involving a lot of planes and a major stunt. That was okay with me. I was sick of hanging around Hollywood. Maybe Blue would be back and and in any case it would be worth money.

The other was a plain envelope with a San Francisco postmark. I didn't know a soul in San Francisco; well, a few girls perhaps, but I doubted that any of them could write. The envelope was addressed to Aussie Air: the sheet of paper inside contained a brief message. Short enough for me to remember it word for word all these years later. It read:

Richard Browning Esq.,
Encino,
California, USA.

Dear Sir,

I would be glad if you would contact me at the address given below as soon as possible after Friday next. You will learn things that vitally concern you.

The note was signed 'Rupert P. MacKnight'.

CHAPTER TWENTY TWO

That was one of the worst nights of my life – comparable to the one I spent in the dormitory at Dudleigh Grammar while the headmaster decided whether to prosecute me for fraud or simply expel me. It was as bad as the night in 1917 in France when I communed with the rats and lice in the trenches while I made up my mind to desert. The very name MacKnight struck terror. My wife, Elizabeth, could put me in gaol or get me deported from America. Worse, she might want me to live with her again.

I dreamt of suffocating under that mountain of white flesh and I woke up yelling. Then I dreamt of her father, he was a dried-up stick of a man in the dream, ranting about drink and tobacco and refusing me both as I crawled on my hands and knees across bare boards, pleading with him. Each time I woke up I smoked furiously and had a drink, so I was in a bad state by morning.

Somehow, I steadied myself enough to report for work. I drank a gallon of black coffee and took some pills Blue had left around the house. 'Shooters', he called them. The coffee and 'shooters' didn't get rid of my anxiety, but they did let me switch my thoughts from the ghastly MacKnights to the dreadful Hughes which was a profitable focus at least.

I realised afterwards that I must have averaged close to seventy miles an hour on the drive to the airfield. I wasn't late, it was just the 'shooters'. The place was crowded with men and cars and planes. Hughes was there, strutting around in plus-fours, half a head taller than anyone else and with that distant, mad look in his eyes. I barged into the middle of the pilots' group wearing full flying gear and feeling, probably for the first time in my life, full of courage and resolution. Without a single constructive idea in my head, I felt I could handle the MacKnights and Hughes and anyone else who happened along. I even felt I could bed Terri.

'What's going on, chaps?' I bellowed. 'Any fun?'

'You could call it that if you was crazy,' Roscoe Turner said grimly. 'See the Gotha over there?'

I looked across the field in the direction he indicated. 'That's not a Gotha. That's a Sikorsky.'

'You know it and I know it,' Turner growled, 'but they don't know it in Iowa. It's *supposed* to be a Gotha. See the Kraut markings?'

I nodded.

'Idea is we shoot up the Gotha, she crashes and burns and the Huns are kaput. Got it?'

'Sounds all right,' I said. I lit a cigarette with a rock steady hand.

'Yeah. Except she *spins,* crashes and burns.'

'Christ!' I knew it could be done by a good pilot; he'd have to kick the big bomber into a spin and get out quick. Not much room for error.

'It's a cinch,' one of the pilots said. I looked at him and for a moment almost believed he was right. Al Wilson was one of the most experienced stunt flyers on the film. He could do anything with a plane, the way a cowboy can with a horse. 'It's no problem, I tell you. It's the other job I wouldn't fancy.'

As I say, I was feeling brave, but when Wilson said something was hard it was time to listen, not start sticking your hand in the air. Turner picked up a chalkboard and looked at it. Then he shook his head. 'He'll have to do it some other way. Ain't nobody going to try that.'

I couldn't help it, those damn pills. 'What?' I said.

Wilson took a plug of tobacco from his flying suit and bit off a chunk. 'Someone's got to lie in the fuselage near the rear and let off the smoke pots. He'll have to jump about the same time as me. Want to try it, Kelly?'

I'll never know whether I would have agreed or not. My teeth rattle when I think of it. I believe I had my mouth open to speak but one of the grease monkeys, Phil Jones, got in before me.

'I'll do it!' he said excitedly. 'On one condition.'

'You're crazy, Phil. You can't . . .' Wilson almost swallowed his chew.

'What's the condition?' Turner said quietly. 'Have to tell you, Mr Hughes don't care too much for conditions.'

'Condition is, he lets me fly.'

'And pays you flying dough,' one of the pilots said.

'Screw the money,' Jones snapped. 'I want to fly!'

'It's your neck,' Turner said. 'I'll tell them. Reckon it'll be okay, Phil.'

Jones wiped his greasy hands on his overall. 'Great. Where's the 'chutes, boys?'

There were high, fluffy clouds overhead as the planes took off. I went up in an old Fokker bomber as co-pilot. The plane carried two cameras, mounted on the wing struts and operated by switches from inside the plane. Joe Boyd, the pilot, and I had separate seats in front and the cameraman was crammed into a back compartment with James Whale. Hughes was in an observation plane circling a hundred feet above the action.

Still pilled-up and confident, I was getting set to enjoy the ride and the stunt when I heard the camera operator groan. The Fokker had a finely tuned engine and I could hear above its noise if I twisted myself around towards the back.

'What's wrong? What? What?' Whale yelled.

'Friggin' camera won't work.'

'Whaddya mean won't work? Which? Which?'

'The left.' He jiggled the switch on the end of its cable like a craps player about to throw. 'It's dead.'

'Gimme that!' Whale grabbed the switch and worked it frantically. 'Oh, Christ,' he wailed. 'We need that angle. The whole thing is nothing without it. Nothing!' He looked at me. 'Can we signal to Wilson that we've got a fuck up? Need some time?'

'I'll ask.' I turned, leaned forward and put the question to Boyd. He shook his head. 'Not anticipated. No signals.'

Whale got the message without me having to relate it. His face darkened. 'What's your speciality – stunts?'

'Just a co-pilot,' I said. I was wearing full flying gear as I've said, also a parachute which I liked to wear whenever I was around planes – even if I wasn't necessarily going up.

'Know anything about cameras?'

I was over-confident and unwary. I shrugged. 'A bit.'

'You've got a parachute on. You could crawl out along the wing and fix it.'

'What?'

'It's got a manual switch. Look, it's not far. A few feet is all. And you've got a parachute.'

I was alarmed but I wasn't taking him seriously. He couldn't mean it. 'I've never jumped,' I said. 'What about him?' I pointed to the cameraman.

'Not me, buddy. I'm staying right here.'

'What's going on?' Joe Boyd twisted around and I saw his bushy eyebrows go up under the goggles.

'Camera won't work. Mr Whale wants me to crawl out and switch it on.'

He craned his neck from the cockpit to inspect the left wing. 'Piece of cake,' he said. 'What's he offering?'

'What? What?' Whale yelled.

'Pilot wants to know what you'll pay him to go out there.'

'A grand,' Whale said.

Boyd squirmed in his seat and checked the straps on his chute. 'Hold 'er steady, Dick. Won't take a minute. Where's this switch?'

'Right hand side,' the cameraman said shakily. 'Near the front. Goes down, no, up.'

Boyd grinned. He was one of those lunatics who thought it was fun to do loops and formation flying. Some of the confidence began to drain from me. *I shouldn't have gone up with him,* I thought. Then the fear hit me. I saw everything so clear and sharp and my bones seemed to turn to jelly. If Boyd went out on the wing I'd be flying the plane without another pilot aboard, technically. It was something I'd had a horror of since the first time I took a stick. I felt the sweat break out all over me as I faced the choice – fly solo or crawl out on a wing hundreds of feet above the ground.

'No, wait!' Three pairs of eyes were trained on me as I fought my internal battle. I felt the sensation of falling as I sat there, still buckled into my seat. It was awful, a sort of dropping away of everything and the patchwork of this bit of California rushing up to embrace me, to suck me into itself. Then I imagined myself flying the plane without someone else around to grab the controls. I knew I couldn't do it. I'd freeze, panic and crash the plane for sure. I couldn't explain and there was only one way to stop Boyd – I had to go out on the wing myself.

'I'll go,' I yelled. 'Piece of cake!'

'No need to shout, Dick,' Boyd said. 'Okay, if you want to. But make it snappy, looks like they're getting into place.'

'Hurry! Hurry!' Whale yelped.

I thought of suggesting that he take the parachute and make the crawl himself if he was so keen on getting the shot, but I didn't. I checked the 'chute, unbuckled and hoisted myself over the side of the cockpit onto the wing. The wind whistled past me and plucked at the flaps of my jacket and the ends of the parachute straps. I tried not to look down as I edged along the strut gripping the uprights and moving by inches.

'Okay, Dick?' Boyd yelled. I wondered what he expected me to do – give him a thumbs up? I clung on and inched forward. Luckily, I knew the structure of an aircraft wing – where the strength was and wasn't. Boyd kept the plane rock steady, I'll say that for him, and if I'd been bolder I could have got out and back to the camera in a matter of seconds.

'Hurry! Hurry up!' This was Whale shouting as I crept forward. My stomach had left for the ground long ago; I had none of the pill confidence left. I was all on my own and making a hash of it. I was close to freezing when the plane listed a little and I had to grab harder. I looked down.

Wisps of cloud floated just below me. I could see roads, some of them snaking across the landscape, others ruler-straight. The roads were yellow, I don't know why. The worst thing was the feeling of speed – the ground seemed to be moving rapidly and not in any uniform way. The blades of the propeller were slicing up the air and they seemed to be only inches away. Then, in a horrible surge, a lurching, head-pounding rush, the wish to leap out into space took hold of me. I wanted to dive towards the ground and be swallowed up. I ground my teeth, clawed my way forward and moved the switch on the camera.

I heard the cameraman yell and felt Boyd correct as a wind gust hit the plane, but I have no memory at all of getting back into my seat. One minute I was out on the wing, the next I was in the cockpit fumbling with buckles.

'Well done,' Whale said. Then he laughed, 'You should've asked for the grand.'

I didn't care. I was too busy feeling the different parts of my body reuniting as the all-over trembling abated.

'We're set, Mr Whale,' the cameraman said.

'You know the plan,' Whale rasped. 'Follow it. You sure the camera's right?'

'Hundred per cent. Here we go. Mr Kelly, will you tell Mr Boyd we're shooting?'

It had been a long time, it seemed, since I'd heard such respect in a man's voice. Heroes must hear it all the time but you learn to live without it. I grunted something to Boyd who nodded and banked left.

The mock Gotha lumbered through the skies and the fighters burst out of the clouds and began to buzz around it like angry wasps. Wilson made a few turns and lost height; the fighters came in firing. During the war, don't ask me how, they'd devised a way for planes to shoot forward, through the props. Before that it had been all back and sideways firing which was much less spectacular and effective. Now the fighters buzzed and blazed, raking the bomber from end to end. Smoke billowed from the Gotha; Wilson kicked it into a spin and jumped.

Everyone in my plane cheered as we saw the 'chute open. I could hear the camera whirring and Whale was sucking air in through his teeth as he watched the bomber spin towards the ground. Joe Boyd was singing some terrible fly-boy song –

Ten thousand feet up in the air

I haven't got a single care

or something like that. The bomber came down in a rocky field, still spinning, seemingly gaining speed. It hit and a sheet of flame ripped through it burning like a beacon in a mass of dense, dark smoke.

I spotted Hughes' scout plane cruising above us and then everything seemed to go crazy. Hughes' plane swooped towards the ground and the fighters circled, broke pattern and regrouped and began to peel off, all trying to find landing spots at once. I had my eye on Hughes' plane. It was making for the place where the bomber was burning.

'Christ,' I said. 'He's going to land on top of it.' I was very peeved. I'd been looking forward to getting down and being the hero of the hour. A thousand bucks was nothing to Hughes; I didn't see why I shouldn't have it, and a gallon of whisky and a lot of back-slapping besides. Now it looked as if nobody would care. 'What the hell's going on?' I yelled at Whale.

The Fokker's motor was quiet as Boyd made a stately descent but I could still barely hear what he said he spoke so quietly.

'Only one 'chute opened. Phil went down with the plane.'

CHAPTER TWENTY THREE

There was a hell of a flap on the ground. Hughes had risked life and limb (his and his pilot's) to land on a rock-strewn stretch near the crashed Sikorsky. But it was no use; the plane was burning and Jones was already dead when they got to him. It was all shouts and clanging bells; the heroism of yours truly got completely lost in the shuffle. Al Wilson had landed soft as a feather a mile away and when he got out of the car that had brought him to the crash everyone surrounded him, babbling questions.

'What happened, Al?'

'Did he get stuck, Al?'

Wilson was white-faced and shaking. Someone gave him a cigarette and he had trouble holding his mouth steady enough to get it lit.

'Why didn't he jump, Al?'

Wilson shrugged and drew on his cigarette. 'I don't know,' he said. 'I wasn't there.'

Hughes left the scene pretty quickly but Whale was on the job. I saw him checking with the cameramen from the different planes. Each nodded. They'd got the shot.

'That makes four,' Joe Boyd said as we tied down the Spad. 'Counting the three pilots got killed before. How much d'they reckon this thing's gonna cost?'

'I heard four million.'

He shook his head. 'Not worth it. Look, Dick,' he leaned towards me and I smelt the liquor on his breath. I was glad I hadn't known about *that* when we went up. 'We should hit Whale for the grand on that wing-walking stunt.'

'We?'

'Sure. You need a witness, bit of pressure applied. Specially after what's happened. If you're willing to split it with me I'll get to work on it.'

That was Hollywood for you – in mourning one minute and counting cash the next. But there was no way to beat the system. 'OK, Joe,' I said. 'Fifty-fifty.'

Along with some of the other fliers and members of the film crew we went drinking at a roadhouse on Sunset. Joe was secretly celebrating his five hundred; the others were holding a wake for Phil Jones; I was wishing I had Terri's shoulder to cry on and trying not to think about meeting up with anyone named MacKnight. We made an afternoon, an evening and a night of it. I don't remember many details. There was a lot of bad singing and cursing of Hughes which only stopped when an assistant editor who was rough-cutting the rushes raised his glass in a toast.

'Gennlemen,' he said, 'le's drink a toas' to a four million dollar turkey.'

Everyone around the table fell silent. We'd all put a lot of work into the picture and to even the drunkest of us four men's lives and four million bucks meant something.

'Whaddya mean, Ed?' Boyd rasped. 'You're cuttin' the stuff, ain't ya? You mean to tell us it's no good?'

''S good. 'S great. Wunnerful action. Brrroooowwww . . .' He emptied his glass and buzzed the table with it. Boyd grabbed his hand.

'What the hell d'you mean by calling it a turkey, then?'

The editor shook free and poured another drink from the litter of bottles on the table. 'It's magnif'cent film. But it's silent! Mar'my words. By the time it's released, silent films won' be worth a dime.'

He burst into laughter and everyone joined in. They toasted the turkey and someone tried to order one from the kitchen. The party got a new lease of life from that moment. It was as if the failure of the film was the right monument to the dead men – don't ask me why. You can see that Howard Hughes hadn't exactly won the hearts and minds of the people who worked for him.

I woke up on the back seat of the Dodge. The flies' buzzing sounded as loud as the planes in a *Hell's Angels'* dogfight and my mouth felt as if I'd been drinking aviation fuel. It was noon; I'd parked the Dodge any old how the night before and now I wished I'd put it under a tree. The sun was high and I badly needed a drink. I also needed some courage because, mysteriously, a plan of action had come to me through the booze haze sometime in the last twelve hours. It was Thursday; MacKnight had said to contact him after Friday but only an idiot gives an adversary the upper hand like that. At the very least I'd take a look at Mr MacKnight before we met and, with any luck, I'd hit on a way to neutralise him.

The address was Highland Avenue, way back down the Boulevard. I found a pair of sunglasses in the car, hooked them on with difficulty, nearly poking an eye out, and drove west. In those days that part of Hollywood was a mixture of business and residential. It wasn't a place you would go to if you had a lot of money but neither would you fit in if you had none. That's the worst kind of person to deal with: someone who has *some* money always wants more. I felt very shaky; there were various MacKnights at my wedding and very big, strapping chaps some of them had been. Others, cousins and such, were positively weedy. There were young and old among them; I was hoping for one of the old, weedy ones.

I stopped somewhere near Las Palmas and bought a bottle at a place I knew would sell a man a bottle if he needed it badly enough and had enough money. I don't remember what was in it, maybe there was no name for it, but I do remember that there was a good few swallows less of it by the time I got to the bungalow court on Highland Avenue which MacKnight had given as his address.

The smallish houses were situated around a wild, rather overgrown patch of garden. Grass had broken through the gravel drive in spots, and trees and creeper vines couldn't quite conceal the fact that paint was peeling off wood. It was the sort of place the studios parked actors they couldn't use but didn't want to discard, or where companies kept space for their travelling salesmen or where divorced wives lived. Or blackmailers. Cash for the rent and clear away your own bottles.

I snooped, located the right bungalow and prowled around it. No car, no bottles out back, no mail in the box. The place looked empty but not uninhabited; there was something about it, the half-drawn blinds on some windows, the flattened grass beside the path (that time with the Indians hadn't been entirely wasted) that indicated occupancy. I steeled myself to break in at the rickety-looking back window.

'Dick Browning?'

Everything about the sound made me jump – the Australian tone, the confidence and, above all, the closeness. I was standing by a tree looking at the back of the house and he was by another tree not twenty feet away. It's an odd thing but I remember that the trees were gums. They're all over California. He was just as I'd feared – six foot two if an inch, with a chin like a rock. Huge shoulders; a rowing eights type; they tend to be fiercely family-minded and unimaginative. The white suit and hand-painted tie probably weren't what they were wearing in Melbourne that year, but he was still a figure of terror and retribution to me.

'Ah,' I said.

He shoved a great red, meaty paw at me. 'Rupe MacKnight.' I caught just a faint tang of Californian under the Australian tone. It became stronger when he added, 'Attorney at law.'

'Jesus,' I said, 'and you'd be Elizabeth's . . . ?'

'Cousin.' He'd been gripping my hand in a circulation-cutting way all this time, now he let it drop. 'Her father and mine are brothers. You ever meet your Uncle Angus? Uncle by marriage, that is? He wasn't at the wedding.'

I shook my head.

'A real bastard,' MacKnight said. 'Well, let's go inside and get to it. We've got a lot to talk about.'

In fact I was thinking of running, but by this time he had his heavy arm around my shoulders and was steering me towards the front of the house. He let himself in, talking and shoulder-gripping the whole time; I wasn't sure but I thought he might be frisking me.

'Got a jug back here.' He made a mock-conspiratorial skip as we passed from the hallway into the kitchen. 'I figure you for a drinking man.' He was getting more Californian by the second. If I'd been wiser in the ways of the world I'd have considered recruiting him to my side. It's been my experience that men and women who can't decide which nationality they are can be 'turned', as the intelligence people say. I . . . [The tape becomes indistinct at this point as Browning breaks off. The tape apparently still ran for a time but attempts to reconstruct what was recorded have so far failed. At a guess, Browning was about to allude to some experience in 'the intelligence community' but thought better of it and moved back from the microphone. It is possible that audible references to this as yet unsuspected aspect of his life history may emerge in later tapes. Ed.]

We went out to a garden bench, table and chairs under pine trees at the back of the house. MacKnight carried the pottery jug by the handle. I suppose I could have disappeared into the trees at this point but there were a number of things against that. In the first place, he didn't appear violent. Secondly, he knew me by sight and would be able to find me if he tried. Third, there was a comforting sloshing sound in the jug. Fourth, though fearful, I was curious and, despite myself, ready to hear news from home.

'Take a seat, Mr Browning, sir. Be a while since anyone called you that, I'll bet.'

I sat on one of the seats, lit a Camel and didn't say anything. MacKnight took a swig from the jug, wiped the lip with the back of his hand and passed it over. I had a cautious belt.

'Biding your time, I see. That's wise.' He reached into the inside pocket of his jacket and extracted a fat wallet. From one of its compartments he extracted a newspaper cutting. We exchanged – the jug for the cutting. The clipping was from the Melbourne *Argus* and it showed the immediate aftermath of Hughes' crash in the Morse. I was there among the helping hands; full face, looking up, clipped moustache, no goggles, no helmet. Just good old Dick Browning as large as life.

I heard the jug slosh as MacKnight lowered it; I reached out blindly and he hooked my finger through the handle.

'Elizabeth saw the picture and got in touch with me. She knew I'd opened a practice in these parts. Be years since we met, mind.' He grinned. "Bout the same for you, I'd guess. How *did* you get to America?'

I let the corn liquor slide down while my mind raced back over my entrances and exits from America. I was confused. By plane was it? No, mule. Or was it boat? Yes, that was it.

'Stowaway,' I muttered.

'Illegal entry. My God, has she got the goods on you!'

'What d'you mean?'

'Why we've been in correspondence some time now. Lot of family gossip, of course, but also tin tacks. Elizabeth is discreet about it but I'm given to understand that you could face charges back home – civil and military.'

'Civil?'

He beckoned for the jug. I'd left the cigarettes on the table and he shook one out and examined it in his thick, blunt fingers. 'Matter of assault on a railway train. Serious injuries resulting. Also fraud proceedings in respect of . . . ah . . . Brown Knight Films, I believe.'

'That'd be old Campbell's doing,' I said bitterly.

'Very likely. But you see the spot you're in. You've as good as admitted illegal entry . . .'

'No, I . . .'

He held up his hand. 'Doesn't matter. Working under a false name. Tax problems for sure. And I've done a little sniffing Dick, old son. There's a matter of a yacht.'

'Jesus.'

'I'm glad you dropped by early. Gives us a bit more time to sort things out. Now, Elizabeth's a slighted woman, very badly damaged emotionally and so on. You follow me.'

I stubbed out my cigarette and lit another. MacKnight replaced the one he'd taken. 'No,' I said.

'I'm sure you do. Deserting a woman in that state . . .'

'State? What the hell d'you mean? New South Wales? She was a train ride from home, sort of.'

'She was pregnant, Dick.'

'Pregnant?'

'You're the father of a child who's, let me see, going on eight now, or is it nine.'

My hand shook as I took the jug. 'Boy or girl?'

'You're not to know. Elizabeth wants a divorce.'

I swallowed gratefully. 'Well, of course, after all this time she . . .'

'And money.'

'Money?'

'Twenty five thousand dollars to be exact. That's your own true wife's price for not dumping you in the shit.'

CHAPTER TWENTY FOUR

It was just the sort of unreasonable demand Elizabeth would make. Where the hell would I get twenty-five thousand dollars? MacKnight took out a handkerchief and mopped his face. We were half in the sun and the day was warm. I was sweating inside my leather jacket. I peeled it off and some papers fell out of the pocket. MacKnight leaned forward quickly and grabbed them.

'Hey,' I said.

'Come, come, cousin. What do we have here?'

There was a cheque book and a few other bits of Aussie Air paperwork – fuel bills and the like. MacKnight smiled as he handed them back. 'Told you I'd done some sniffing. Not a bad little concern, this company of yours. Your interest's worth a few dollars, I'd say.'

The liquor had soothed the hangover and the tobacco slowly unravelled my nerves. *Perhaps things weren't too bad after all,* I thought. *Divorce from Elizabeth – that was a plus, and maybe I could extract some promise of silence from her as part of the deal. An affidavit even. And the work on the picture was coming to an end. I wasn't sure that I wanted to be part of an expanded Aussie Air. Maybe it was time to sell out. How much was the thing worth?* Then a wave of excitement hit me. *Divorced from Elizabeth, I could marry Terri! Maybe that was what she was holding out for all along.* Things began to look rosy. I had another drink. *A child in Australia, eh? One I'd never seen and probably never would see. Well, you can't have everything.*

'Mr MacKnight,' I said. 'I think we can do business.'

We finished the jug and in the process I found that MacKnight was not a bad chap. Grasping and ambitious, of course, but all the MacKnights were like that. He had no love of the clan himself and had come to the States to get away from them.

'Father wanted me to be a stock and station agent. C'n you imagine that?'

I looked at his white suit, now a little grubby around the edges from spilt liquor and the ash from the small, black cigars he had begun smoking. He was wearing wingtip shoes, I noticed, and silk socks.

'No,' I said. 'I can't. More of a city man, I'd say.'

''S right. Bloody well right. Rupert MacKnight doesn't want shit on his boots. Wants t'walk on carpet, and sit on chairs not bloody horses. Hate horses, don't you?'

'No. Can't say that. Horses are fine with me.'

He made a circular motion with his hand. 'All right running around a track. Money on 'em. *That's* all right. You go to the track, Dick?'

I hadn't in a good long time and when I said so nothing would do but that we went that afternoon. I protested but I had nothing better to do really. MacKnight splashed water on his face which seemed to sober him. He lent me a clean shirt (we were much of a size for sleeve length) and off we went to Santa Monica in the Dodge. I cashed a cheque on the way because Rupe said he didn't have any ready money on him.

'Where's your office?' I asked.

'Downtown.' I was driving and shouldn't have been as I was still too drunk. I was giving the road all my attention or I wouldn't have been satisfied with the answer.

At the track Rupe borrowed some money and we drank steadily. Chaplin was there, I recall, and a few lesser lights such as Charlie

Farrell and Marie Dressler.[28] I offered to introduce MacKnight to Farrell but he didn't seem interested.

'Fairbanks isn't here, is he?'

Christ, I hope not, I thought. I shot an anxious look up to the grandstand and across the sea of faces clustered in the betting ring. There was an aura around Fairbanks, he'd stand out in any crowd no matter how big. 'No, he's not here. Charlie's good fun, he . . .'

'Gotta gamble,' MacKnight roared. People heard him above the hum of odds-calculating and winnings-collecting voices and turned to look. 'Gambling man, Dick. Backed Spearfelt inna Cup.[29] Ten to one. You on it?'

'No. Look, Rupe, take it easy. Put that bloody flask away. You can't do that here.'

'Corsican. Napoleon brandy. Get it? Napoleon. Corsican. Hah, hah. Like this Tijuana Lass inna third. Been to Tijuana, Dick? Course you have. Chap like you. Girls like that . . .'

This set MacKnight off on a long spiel about brothels from Sydney to San Francisco. Interesting enough talk in its way and I had a bit to say on the subject, although nothing very recent. I was more interested in trying to get details about Elizabeth and my child from him, but either he wasn't as drunk as he made out or he didn't know much, because I learned nothing. MacKnight was a great newspaper reader though and he was able to fill me in on things that had happened in Australia since my cover-of-darkness departure.

'Hear about the forty-four hour week?' he said, sometime after Tijuana Lass had finished next to last.

'No. What's that?'

'Lang[30] got in in New South. Passed a law – forty-four hour week.'

'Christ,' I said, 'that's Communism, near enough.'

'Plenty of them around too,' he said darkly. 'What d'you like in the next?'

'Nothing. What're Elizabeth's . . . ah, circumstances?'

'Y'mean how's she fixed for cash?' He tilted the flask, concealing it in his meaty hands. 'Be better if she was in New South.'

'How's that?'

'Got a law there gives an allowance to parents. So much per kid.'

'God, the micks'll be breeding like rabbits.'

'Right. Trade Unions've formed their own Parliament – ACTU. Land o' the free, home o' the . . . Whaddya like again in the next?'

Rupe had more losses than wins so that he was into me for more than fifty bucks when we left the track. Maybe this was what made me stick with him, maybe I just wanted the company, but we ended up making a night and day of it and another night. I can't remember all the places we went – low dives mostly, speakeasies and gin joints as our shirts wilted and our tongues got furrier. Some of what happened came back to me later: I remember Mexican girls and tequila . . . no, it was all too vague. What I can say is that I was lying on the couch in the front room of MacKnight's bungalow when I felt something burning my hand. I yelled and jerked awake and MacKnight came lumbering naked into the room. He was fatter than I'd thought and he looked ghastly with a dark shadow all over a ghostly pale, flabby face.

'What? What?' he roared.

I found that my hand was in the middle of a pot in which stood a big cactus plant. Several cactus spines were half an inch or so into my flesh. MacKnight laughed. The sound nearly took my head off but didn't seem to bother him. Again the thought came dimly to me that he couldn't have been as drunk as he seemed.

'You stole that from the whorehouse,' he said. 'They put something on the spikes – chilli or something.'

I pulled my hand free and rubbed the spreading red blotches. 'Christ,' I said. 'Who drove home?'

'Me.' He seemed strangely business-like, for all the signs of high alcohol and tobacco intake along with bad food and sleep. 'I'll make some coffee,' he said. 'Fancy breakfast?'

I shuddered and slid back down on the couch. Everything hurt, from head to hand and down the legs to the feet. One foot, I discovered was bare; the shoe and sock were beside the couch. The lace on the other shoe was undone – that must have been as far as I'd got. *Commendable try, Browning,* I thought, *I'm surprised your pants aren't wet.*

Rupe came in with a pot of coffee, two cups and a bowl of breakfast cereal. He'd shaved and washed himself, changed his shirt and combed his hair. For the first time I noticed that he had very white teeth. They helped him to look healthy and normal as he wolfed down the cereal.

'Have a cup,' he said. 'You'll feel better.'

'Would you mind pouring? I don't think I can manage.'

He smiled, put his bowl down carefully and poured the coffee. I got some down and looked at him as he munched happily.

'How come you're so chipper?' I said. 'Seems to me you owe me money.'

He shook his head. 'Not me.'

'Come on! Jesus!' Shouting hurt my head. I drank some more coffee and tried for a calmer tone. 'I cashed cheques, I . . .'

'You signed a paper, son.' He took a sheet of paper from his shirt pocket, unfolded it and held it out for me to read. I tried but shook my head.

'It says: I, Richard Kelly, also known as Browning, willingly avow that no financial obligations are entailed in my dealings with Rupert B. MacKnight, Attorney at Law, other than those stipulated in such signed and duly witnessed contracts as may exist.'

'What the hell does that mean?'

'You'll note the witnesses' signatures.'

I tried to focus on the paper before he snatched it away. 'The madam was one,' he said. 'Not so good perhaps, but the other signature is okay. He's a distinguished member of the California bar. A few of his colleagues were there, too. I took you to the right place.'

I was beginning to locate things – thoughts and feelings even – in the midst of pain and confusion. 'All this to clear a few bets, a few bar and whorehouse tabs? I don't get it.'

He shook his head and poured himself some coffee. After a quick sip he heaved himself up. 'Just wait there, Richard. Something to show you.'

I drank some coffee and wanted a cigarette but there was nothing in my pockets. Absolutely nothing. When MacKnight came back he was carrying a Smith & Wesson .38 and some folded, legal-looking papers. He put the gun by his right hand and smoothed the papers with his left. 'You signed a good deal last night, Richard. Tequila's like that, I've found. Leaves a man with motor control but no will.'

'Signed?'

'And witnessed by the aforementioned colleagues.'

'Signed what?'

'An agreement to pay Elizabeth Browning, née MacKnight, the sum of twenty-five thousand dollars in lieu of marital support, duties, child maintenance, etc.'

There goes my affidavit, I thought. 'What else?'

'A transfer of all interests in the firm of Aussie Air to Yarra Enterprises Ltd., in return for and in due payment of all fees pertaining to the conducting of all transactions in respect of the said Elizabeth MacKnight. I may say that I am the principal of Yarra Enterprises.'

'You bastard,' I said.

He nodded. 'Once a MacKnight, Dick, always a MacKnight.'

CHAPTER TWENTY FIVE

If I had been a violently disposed sort of chap I'd have hit him, but I'm not, and in my time I've seen too much violence rebound on the perpetrator to think it's a good strategy. In tight corners I tend to lick my wounds, look around for allies and get ready to run. Besides, MacKnight was considerably bigger than me and he looked a lot fresher. He scribbled his telephone number on the back of a card, gave it to me and showed me the door.

'Talk to your partner, Dick. Tell him how you're fixed although I suppose you'll doctor the details a bit. Anyway,' here he slapped me on the back hard enough to send me reeling and perhaps to give me the idea that his weight was not only legal, 'you can tell him Aussie Air doesn't have to change a thing. I'm as Australian as . . .'

'A Sydney Harbour shark?'

He roared and hit me again. 'Very good, Dick. Very good. Tell you what, I'll come around myself, say about four, to talk things over with you and Tait. I hear he got back yesterday.'

I was off the porch now, blinking in the sunlight and trying to see my car. 'How could you hear anything yesterday?' I said. 'You were drunk all day.'

'I got to the phone a couple of times, mate. Don't you worry. See you at four, Dick. I know where you live.'

I nodded and stumbled towards the car which I'd located, parked skew-whiff, by the gate. MacKnight followed me and gripped my shoulder. 'No funny business, Dick. It's all watertight and legal and you're a deserter, an illegal alien with criminal charges against you. You haven't a leg to stand on.'

On the drive to Encino I thought about possible allies. Blue? He'd been cool lately for no reason I could fathom. With all the talk of oil contracts and such, he might welcome lawyer MacKnight as a partner instead of two-pilot Browning. Terri? I'd hardly seen her in weeks. I could offer to marry her if the deal with MacKnight went through and then I could offer her empty pockets and fresh air. Silkstein? He was interested in only one thing – his ten per cent. I'd heard him talk about former clients, failed actors, drunks and hop heads who got banned from the studios. I'd seen him hang up, stony-faced, on a weeping actress who'd managed to get her call past Miss Dupre.

'This is a tough business, Dick,' he said. 'You know how I look at it? Ten per cent of sumthin' ain't much an' a hunnert per cent of nuthin' is nuthin'.'

I couldn't expect any help from Silkstein.

The immediate problem was lack of money and low gas in the Dodge. I pulled in at a bank on the other side of Las Palmas and got a hell of a surprise when the teller wouldn't cash my cheque. I was unshaven and rumpled, true, but this was California and some millionaires looked that way when it pleased them.

'I'm sorry, sir,' the teller said. He smoothed his hair down and continued the gesture through to his moustache. 'We can't cash your cheque for that amount at this branch. You'll have to take it to Encino.'

'I need to buy gas to *get* to Encino.'

'I'm sorry, sir.' He didn't look sorry. I felt anger rising in me and tried to keep calm.

'I've cashed cheques at other branches before without trouble. What's new?'

'There *is* a new policy. With all the share speculation that's been going on, personal cheques have become, shall we say, a little suspect.' He gave me a toothy grin. 'You could cash a dud cheque, rush out and buy RCA stock and make a killing in a half hour.'

I ignored the cough from the person in the line behind me. 'Do I look as if I'm going to buy RCA stock?'

'No, sir. But that hardly helps your case.'

A wise guy, I thought. The anger rose further and I was talking through gritted teeth now. 'There must be a way.'

'We-ll, I could telephone to the Encino branch . . .'

'That's it!'

'Have you got the cost of the call?'

This was in the days before bullet-proof glass around bank tellers. He was about five and half feet tall and a hundred pounds. I could've reached over and shaken his teeth out and he knew it. 'You can deduct the call from the withdrawal,' I said.

'Yes, sir.'

He scurried off and I continued to ignore the coughing and shuffling behind me. He returned and flipped my cheque to me, standing well back from the counter. 'There are no funds in this account!'

'But . . .'

'I'm sorry, sir, you'll have to discuss it in Encino. Stand aside, please. Next in line, thank you.'

Banks are bad places to feel bad in and the worst way to feel in a bank is poor. I shuffled away to make room for the folks with money in their accounts and went back out to the car. I wasn't too worried about the empty account. Blue and Terri could write cheques on it and it sometimes happened, particularly when we weren't conferring often as we weren't just then, that funds dipped low. It seemed more important that I was hungry and thirsty and out of cigarettes but at least I had the car. Cars are like banks – they tend to hold money in them when there's money about. I dug under the seats, into every compartment and fold, and came up with a little over two dollars. It was enough for gas, cigarettes, a sandwich and a near beer – hard to believe nowadays but it's true.

As it turned out, it was also enough for a newspaper to read while I ate, smoked and digested in a cafe two doors from the bank. I knew I was delaying getting back to the house and talking to Blue and Terri about my problems, but why not? Anyone who hurries towards his problems is an idiot in my book. You never know what can happen and how useful a little time can be. Think how useful a couple of seconds were to Tunney in Chicago.[31]

This thought sent me to the sports pages. An enquiry was on into the running of Tijuana Lass at Santa Monica two days before. The horse had been doped, apparently – looked like MacKnight had got his signals wrong. This cheered me up until I remembered that it was my money he'd lost. They were still looking for a heavy-weight champion following Tunney's retirement. There was talk of Schmeling which was all right with me, the war was a long time over. I regretted that I'd never seen Dempsey fight. Maybe he'd make a comeback and I could get to see him – I was pretty sure he could make liverwurst out of Schmeling.

Business was still booming. There was nothing in the paper about banks being careful about cheques. There was trouble about Al Wilson and the stunt in *Hell's Angels.* Looked like Wilson would lose his pilot's licence. That seemed tough but it was great publicity for Hughes and the movie. A real live death scene – it'd pack 'em in, almost as good as a hanging. That led me to regional news. There were elections here and there and Al Capone was in gaol for carrying a concealed weapon. That *was* news – I'd never heard of him bother-ing to conceal one before.

'Another drink, buddy?' He didn't know that I'd have two cents in my pocket after I'd bought the gas. I stubbed out my cigarette and stood.

'No, thanks, but here, take the paper. I'm through with it.'

'Gee, thanks. I can check on my Montgomery Ward stock.' He was a fat man with no teeth and a dirty apron but he *could* have been serious. That's how things were in 1929.

'Fifty cents worth of regular, please.'

'You won't get out of the state on that, Mac.'

This was the gas station attendant, a kid with red hair like Blue's and a cocky grin. 'What?' I said. 'Who the hell's getting out of the state?' I was too edgy to get the joke.

'Take it easy, mister. No need to blow your top.'

'Check the air.'

In my scramblings around for change in the car I'd come across its registration papers. Like the house and the planes and the cheque books, it belonged to Aussie Air. As I drove through the warm afternoon I thought of all the Company papers I'd signed and witnessed – transfers of this, leases of that – I didn't pay much attention because businesss bored me. But now I reflected on what the company might be worth and whether there could be any change over me for me even if the deal with MacKnight held. There *had* to be – America was booming, fortunes were being made.

A Studebaker shot across an intersection in front of me just before I reached the driveway to the house. I braked and yelled, dropped my cigarette into my lap and rabbit-hopped the rest of the distance. I had a hole in my trousers, a powerful thirst for some real liquor and a drumming headache when I opened the door to the house. Before I went in I turned and looked around the front lawn. It was overgrown as usual; the garden was drying out in patches as usual; the earth around the rose bush nearest the porch was littered with my cigarette butts the way it always was. But something was different. I shaded my eyes and squinted. No bottles in the hammock. No bottles anywhere. The place had been cleaned up.

Terri's back, I thought. The woman's touch! Clean dishes and dry towels in the bathroom. I opened the door and walked in to silence except for buzzing flies, and emptiness, apart from the furniture that had been in the house when we rented it.

'Hello!' I called. 'Hey, Dick's back! Aussie Air forever!'

There was no reply. Silence took up all the available space. I stumbled down the passageway into the kitchen. There was a bottle of Canadian whisky in the middle of the table and propped up against it was a white envelope with 'Dick' written on it in Terri's neat, precise hand.

CHAPTER TWENTY SIX

I've kept that letter for fifty years and I have it in front of me now. It reads:

Dear Dick,

Maybe you had better sit down and pour yourself a shot because this is going to come as a surprise to you. We've sold the Company to one of Hughes' corporations. When I say sold I mean it – lock, stock and barrel. Everything.

We're sorry to deceive you like this but there was no other way. You have to admit that Blue and I did 99% of the work so it's only fair that we should get the benefit. Or maybe it isn't fair but that's the way it is. Blue says that tough times are coming for this country and it's time to get out. He said you'd never understand or not quickly enough to do what was necessary, so we had you sign your interest over to us. It's all legal. Blue says you're a survivor which is right and I know you'll get over this.

The lease on the house runs out at the end of the week. All the bills are paid. We made sure not to leave you with any of the Company's debts. We're going to South . . . well, it could be America or Australia or Africa. It's better you don't know.

That's all there is to say, Dick. We were prepared to face you and tell you this and about the wedding but you weren't around and perhaps it's better this way.

Goodbye and good luck.

yours,

Terri Tait.

It was a shock all right. I absorbed it slowly along with the whisky, sitting alone in the quiet kitchen with the light gradually dimming outside. The signature was a hard blow in itself. Why hadn't I seen it? Blue dropping his women, Terri never around, both of them away on trips. It was obvious, but I've always been too trusting of people I like. It's one of my great weaknesses – probably as bad as my habit of totally mistrusting people I don't like. As for signing myself into the poorhouse, I wasn't surprised at that and it wasn't the last time it happened. I've signed away fortunes; I remember when I . . . [Browning, sounding rather drunk, breaks off at this point and mutters the names of film producers such as Darryl Zanuck and Samuel Goldwyn. He also mentions the Knopf publishing house which may be a clue to an attempt to place his memoirs. The editorial department of the Knopf company, however, has no record of a manuscript submitted by Browning nor of any significant correspondence. Ed.]

I read the letter over a couple of times and wandered through the house. Mr and Mrs Tait had taken everything they owned and left me with the clothes I stood up in, a few more in the closet, more still, all dirty, in the laundry, my camera, some photographs and a couple of packets of Camel. They'd even taken things like the binoculars and the guitar which I could've sworn Blue and I had paid half each for in Chicago. Mind you, I'd probably lost my half of the binoculars to him at poker and I couldn't play the guitar anyway. Blue could. I imagined him serenading Terri on a beach somewhere and I had several more belts of the Canadian to keep the tears at bay.

About dusk I wandered out of the house with the vague idea of driving into Los Angeles to sell the car. I knew I was drunk but I thought I'd remembered where I'd put the car. No car. I lurched down the driveway and found a card on the ground near the oilspots. It was from the Hughes Transport Services Company and it informed me that possession had been taken of one 1928 Dodge convertible.

I went back into the house. No car, no money, no passport, no house, no job. Just a bottle of whisky, no, half a bottle of whisky and some cigarettes. And some dirty clothes. It was a very low tide; one of those times when you wonder why you left home and your wife. Wife! That set the alarm bells ringing. I was in a hell of a spot I realised, having agreed to dispose of something I didn't have. I knew how Elizabeth would feel about that. Who was it said, 'Don't get mad, get even?' Elizabeth would get both and Rupe MacKnight would help her all the way. If Aussie Air had been attractive to Hughes it must have been worth something. Rupe wasn't likely to be a good loser.

I slumped down at the table, poured another drink and raised the glass. 'Here's to friendship,' I said, 'and women and Howard bloody Hughes. Fuck 'em all!' I drank and poured again. I was trying to think of another toast when the telephone rang. I stumbled up and through to the living room.

'Hullo. Who the hell's this? There's no one here. There's nothing . . .'

'Kelly!' Silkstein's voice scratched at my eardrum.

'Kelly, this is Robert. You drunk, you bum?'

'No. Not yet. Whaddya want?'

'Honest to Christ, I don'know why we bodder wit' you drunken actors. Well, since I'm on the line . . . I gotta tip off the cops are comin' for you.'

That almost sobered me. I saw cold grey walls and bars. 'The police? Why?'

'I dunnu. I got it from some reporter inna bar. Sounded right. Sumthin' about Hughes, sumthin' about your company. You get it sorted out you wanna keep workin' in this town. Got it?'

'You're supposed to help me. You're my agent, you . . .'

'Trouble wit' Hughes I don' need. You get it sorted out you gimme a call. Okay?'

He hung up and I stood with the instrument in my hand wondering what else could go wrong. I picked up my glass, swayed and cracked the edge against a tooth. The tooth broke and I felt a stab of pain that got deeper and more intense by the second. I sipped whisky and my head exploded as the spirit hit the nerve.

'Oh, God!' I slid to the floor and the phone rang again. I had my mouth clamped shut and thought about ignoring the phone. What else could it be but more bad news? But I was a tiger for punishment now. I held the listening bit almost at arm's length and croaked into the mouthpiece through clenched teeth.

'Yeah?'

'That you, Kelly?'

'Yeah.'

'This is Joe, Joe Boyd. I got the dough.'

'What?'

'Are you drunk or what. I got your five hundred bucks. Whale paid off for our stunt with the camera.'

'Our stunt?' I opened my mouth to shout and the cold air hit the tooth like an icepick to the back of the skull.

'Okay, okay. Your stunt, but with anyone else flying the plane you'd have been floating down and getting your ass cut up by someone's prop. You want the dough?'

Want it? I needed it as badly as I've ever needed money. 'Look, Joe,' I said, 'I'm in a spot. Where are you?'

He named a bar on the Strip and I thought fast. I had to leave town and the police would watch the trains and buses. I'd done enough drinking with extras to know what you did in LA when you were down on your luck. 'Can you meet me by the trucking yards? Where they recruit the pickers?'

'I suppose so,' Boyd said. 'But why? Five hundred bucks ain't hay.'

'Just meet me there in two hours with the money. I'll need it to pay the cabbie so don't let me down.'

'I didn't let you down when you were out on the wing, did I?' He laughed and I realised that he'd already started to work through the money. I had to hope he'd stay sober enough to make the meeting and that he'd have some money left. I was a moving heap of pain as I went around the house collecting up my things and shoving them into a duffel bag. There were angry red blotches on my hand where the cactus spines had gone in and the hand was throbbing nearly as bad as my tooth. I drank whisky on the other side of my mouth, took some aspirin and tried to ignore it. I phoned a cab and nearly choked trying to smoke cigarettes through a crack in my mouth while I waited.

I reached the trucking yards around five in the afternoon. It was still hot and nothing much was moving. There was a smell of rotting fruit and vegetables in the air and paper swirled around the dusty yards. The cabbie was suspicious of me because I wouldn't talk. I was on a knife's edge of nerves wondering what I'd do if Boyd didn't show. But he was there, parked in a red Buick in the shade.

'By the Buick,' I grated through clenched teeth.

'Hey, what is this? Some kinda set up? I'll stop here if you don' mind.'

'I do mind.' That let in too much air and I waited for the pain but the liquor and aspirin were working. 'A guy in that car has my money. He pays me and I pay you.'

'I don't like it.'

'It's broad daylight, for Christ sake! You think you're going to get rubbed out for a cab fare?'

'Don' talk like that. OK.'

He stopped beside the Buick. I found Boyd asleep in the front seat. I shook him awake.

'Hey, Joe. Let's have it.' He gave me a wad of tens, twenties and singles. I paid the cabbie and then I counted it. Joe watched me.

'That looks like the only dough you got in the world.'

'That's right.'

'What happened to Blue and your business?'

'Don't ask. You haven't seen me, Joe. OK? You don't know where I am or where I went.'

'Right. I guess you flew off somewhere.'

'That's right. I flew off somewhere. So long, Joe.'

He drove off and I found a shady place behind one of the packing sheds and settled down with my bag to wait. I put some of the small bills in my pocket and the rest in my sock. The whisky and aspirin went on working and I fell asleep.

It was a bad night, full of dreams, shivers and twitching awakenings. And not all of the bad stuff was dreams. Sometime in the night I was jerked awake by a big guy looming over me and prodding me with his boot.

'Hey, you.'

'Wha . . . ? What?'

'Got a light?' His winey breath was sweet and much too close. I fumbled for a match and he punched me in the face with a fist as hard as stone. I slumped back, half-stunned, and felt him go through my pockets. He got the cigarettes and loose money, tried to roll me over and off my bag but gave up when I wouldn't budge. He kicked me in the ribs and slouched away. I lay there gasping with sore ribs to add to my other pains. I felt blood on my face and something hard and sharp in my mouth. I put my hand up to my mouth and found my broken tooth lying under my tongue. I had to smile. Some dentist, but he'd done a neat job.

The men started arriving before dawn. They were dressed warmly for the early morning cold and they drank from bottles in paper bags, smoked, coughed and spat. A miserable collection. I joined a line under a roughly painted cardboard sign that read: 'Grayp pikers'. At dawn the trucks arrived. I was lucky. The turn out was light and the demand for cheap, one-day, no-questions-asked-labour was high. The boss didn't even comment on my bag and the good shoes I had on along with my oldest pants, woollen shirt and flying jacket.

'Evah picked?' he grunted.

As it happened, I had – back in Australia when I'd worked for Robespierre's Wine and Spirits Emporium, I'd spent a few days in one of the local vineyards as a spy for Robespierre who'd wanted to see whether he had anything to fear from the local product. Robespierre himself dealt only in imported lines. 'I've picked,' I said.

'Get in th' truck.'

On the ride out of town I surveyed my companions – winos to a man but mostly thin and hard looking. I doubted that I'd be able to keep up with them. I remembered the actual work, fifteen years or so ago under the Australian sun. It had near crippled me then and I was in no condition for it now. Cautiously, I reached inside my bag for a packet of Camel. I fished it out and every eye – ten pairs, it was – in the truck fell on me.

'Anyone got a match?' Three books of matches appeared – a total of five matches in all. I shook cigarettes out of the packet; the matches were lit and held carefully and soon eleven men were smoking. These were the old days you understand, everyone in long pants smoked and a hell of a lot of the kids in short pants too. There was no lung cancer, no cancer at all . . . [Browning rambles at this point, very drunk. He rants about the Surgeon General's report, warnings on cigarette packets and coughs harshly. The sound of a match being lit can be heard on the tape and also the sound of his wheezy inhalings and exhalations. Ed.]

Anyway, I told them that I had a couple more packs and they could have them if they'd cover for me when I made a break out at the vineyard. A hundred per cent smokers, I'm telling you, and a hundred per cent agreement. We smoked the butts down to the last quarter inch and I sealed the deal by passing around the rest of the Canadian whisky. It was almost a party and I was the guest of honour. Some of the guys had some wine left in their bottles and we passed that around too. Loaves and fishes, it was. I was feeling fine when we arrived at the vineyard. I had a missing tooth but I was feeling no pain.

I stumbled down from the truck and collapsed by the side of the road. I was dumbly aware of hands reaching into my bag and extracting the cigarettes. The winos grinned at each other and moved smoothly off to pick up their buckets. I lay in a sick haze.

'This man's drunk,' the boss said.

'So'm I,' said one of the winos.

The boss looked down at me and kicked me in the ribs where I'd been kicked the night before. 'Ah mean drunk, ah mean cain't-work drunk.'

'Yo,' the wino said.

They went off to work and I vomited a couple of times and finally rolled into a patch of shade and fell asleep. I woke up with flies buzzing and guns going off in my head. I staggered up and lurched along the road carrying my bag and feeling like death. I could hear the sounds of men in the vineyard running with their buckets down the line, cursing when they fell and laughing as they worked. I jumped like a rabbit when a bird-scaring shotgun went off. I was sweating and my shoes and heavy jacket were rubbing me raw when I heard the truck lumbering up the hill behind me. I stuck my thumb out. It was a hay truck, moving slow, smelling sweet. The sun was directly overhead and the driver stopped for me.

'Give y' a rahd if 'n y' c'n jump up at th' back, buddy.'

It must have been noon when I jumped on the hay truck . . . [At this point a knock on a door can be heard on the tape. Browning leaves off taping but does not turn off the machine as was his usual practice when interrupted. The tape continues to run and the following snatch of dialogue can be heard before the tape runs out. Ed.]

Browning: Who's that? Why hello!

Woman: Hello, Richard. You look strange. What's the matter with your mouth?

Browning: Hee, hee. Missing a tooth there. Got m'plate out.

Woman: What're you doing baby?

Browning: C'm in, c'm in. Taping m'memoirs.

Woman: Ooh, that's nice. Am I in them?

Browning: Well . . .

Woman: Wouldn't these be in them, Richard? Come on, you've never had better then these.

Browning: No. I . . .

Woman: That's right. That's my Richard. Ooh, that's right. Richard, what's wrong?

Browning: Oh, Terri.

Woman: Terri! Who the hell's Terri! . . .

APPENDIX

THE MAKING OF *HELL'S ANGELS*

The assistant editor who partied with Browning and the other fliers in the roadhouse on Sunset Boulevard was right. *Hell's Angels* did cost Howard Hughes approximately two million dollars of his own money as well as the the lives of four men. And it was doomed to failure if it was released as a silent film – the success of *The Jazz Singer* had revolutionised the movie industry overnight.

Faced with this crisis a man less tenacious than Hughes and with fewer resources might have caved in, with the result that *Hell's Angels* would become an anachronistic curiosity. Not Hughes. He determined to reshoot all the dialogue scenes and dub in sound for the aerial sequences. Joseph Moncure March, a poet under contract to MGM, was commissioned to write a script. March went further; he jettisoned the structure of the silent version and wrote an entirely new script. A first draft took March only ten days and Hughes liked the result. At that time he was still capable of quick decisions.

But there was a problem. Ben Lyon and James Hall could reproduce their roles without difficulty, but Greta Nissen, who had played the female lead in the silent film, could not. She spoke English with a heavy Norwegian accent.

Hughes got lucky. A theatrical agent named Arthur Landau managed to persuade the film makers, against the evidence of a terrible screen test, that his client Jean Harlow would be right for the part. Harlow performed brilliantly in the seductive role and put everything she had into lines like, 'Do you mind if I slip into something more comfortable?'

By the time the reshooting and sound dubbing was completed *Hell's Angels* had cost $3.8 million, making it the most expensive production to date. The released film was on fifteen thousand feet of celluloid for which 2.5 million feet had been shot. Hughes endured mockery and insult as the film was prepared for release, but he was constantly building a publicity machine to put behind it. He built up curiosity by holding a private showing in advance of the premiere, at Grauman's Chinese Theatre. By private he meant private – only Hughes himself was seated in front of the screen. Louella Parsons, then an aggressive young gossip columnist, sneaked in and refused to leave. Whether Hughes had contrived this or not is unknown.

Planes buzzed the theatres on opening night; stuntmen parachuted onto Hollywood Boulevard and Hughes reputedly offered the owners of the dirigible *Graf Zeppelin* one hundred thousand dollars to advertise the film in the skies above Manhattan. The owners refused but the offer itself was news. With this much push behind it, *Hell's Angels* was a box office smash. Audiences and critics loved the flying and Harlow. Wild, distorted stories spread about Hughes' single-handed creation of the masterpiece. Hughes contradicted nothing.

It has not been possible to investigate records of Hughes' financial operations at this time to check on the purchase of Aussie Air. No mention of the matter is made in Donald Bartlett and James B. Steele's excellent book, *Empire: the life, legend and madness of Howard Hughes* (Norton, 1979), on which the above account is based, but those operations were already vast and complex and such a small transaction might not merit notice. It is worth pointing out, however, that huge amounts of money washed around in the *Hell's Angels* budget. Bonuses of various kinds were paid and conveniently forgotten. Browning's account of the thousand dollars paid to Joe Boyd and himself for the wing-walking exercise is consistent with other evidence about the ways in which the film ate up almost four million dollars. Although Hughes later claimed that the film had been profitable, more sober calculations show that it did not recover its production costs and that Hughes lost about $1.5 million.

NOTES

1. The Royal Canadian Mounted Police were originally organised as the Northwest Mounted Police in 1873, to bring law and order to the Canadian west and protect the settlers against the Indians. The present name was adopted in 1920, just before Browning arrived in Canada. The Mounties, as the constabulary became known, 'always got their man' in countless books and many films. By Browning's time, as he records, more mundane police duties were the order of the day and the RCMP eventually embraced the police forces of all provinces but Ontario and Quebec.

2. The Yukon Territory of north-west Canada is bordered by the Arctic Ocean to the north, the Northwest Territories to the east, British Columbia and Alaska to the south and Alaska to the west. Whitehorse is the capital and Dawson the next most important centre. A gold rush in the 1890s brought more than 30,000 people to the Yukon although the total population, mostly in riverbank settlements, is less than this today. Mining has remained a major activity in the Territory which is 186,299 square miles in area.

3. Captain R. Burton Deane's *Mounted Police Life in Canada: a record of thirty-one-year's service,* (Cassell, London, 1916) is a typical memoir of imperial service. In it Browning would have found much useful information on Mountie

organisation and tradition and an emphasis on loyalty, courage, duty and self-sacrifice.

4. A variety of the highly successful single action Colt army revolver.

5. Modern ethnological opinion does not confirm Sergeant Fraser's theories. Indians and Eskimos are thought to be descended from a common stock of Asian people who entered the American continent from the north.

6. Browning's experiences as a stowaway are documented in the two earlier volumes of his memoirs, *'Box Office' Browning* (1987) and *'Beverly Hills' Browning,* (1988).

7. Jefferson Randolph 'Soapy' Smith, was born in Georgia in 1860, ran away from home when young and became a cowboy and later a gambler. He perfected the three shell game and devised a con in which he and a partner would set up a soap-selling stand in a likely town. Smith would announce that several of the bars of soap on sale had twenty dollars bill inside them. A planted shill would buy a bar and 'discover' the money. The nick-name 'Soapy' stayed with him although he moved up in the gambling world to run his own saloon and gambling establishments, first in Leadville, Colorado and later in Skagway, Alaska. With a band of toughs to enforce his directions, Smith became the virtual ruler of the town, extracting money from the miners in crooked gambling games and by outright holdup on the roads. In 1898 a vigilante committee of Skagway citizens called the Committee of 101, after failing to persuade Smith to release his grip on the town, stormed his saloon and shot him dead.

8. 'Wheat lumper' was an Australian term for a labourer who loaded bags of wheat onto a truck or railway car. The standard weight for a bag of wheat so transported was 112 pounds.

9. Browning refers to the Melbourne Cup, one of the richest horse races in the world. Lord Nolan won the race in 1908, Tulkeroo finished second.

10. Browning was almost certainly making reference to Phillip Island, a tourist attraction in Westernport Bay, Victoria, Australia. The island has a cooler climate but is home to about 4000 so-called 'Fairy Penguins', a species protected by law.

11. As so often, Browning reveals his shaky grasp of even quite recent history. Scott's expedition, on which he perished and during which the badly debilitated Oates sacrificed himself, was to the South Pole in 1910-12.

12. The Burke and Wills expedition left Melbourne in 1860 with the aim of crossing the Australian continent from south to north. The four man party reached the Gulf of Carpentaria in February 1861 but the leader, Robert O'Hara Burke, the second in command, William John Wills and a third member died of exhaustion and starvation on the return journey. One member of the expedition survived due to the attentions of friendly Aborigines. Burke's name in Australian history is synonomous with poor judgement and stubborness.

13. James Joseph 'Gene' Tunney was heavyweight boxing champion of the world from his defeat of Jack Dempsey in 1927 to his retirement in 1928. Charles Augustus Lindbergh, American aviator, made the first solo flight from America to Europe – in the *Spirit of St Louis,* from New York to Paris, in May 1927.

14. Australian for scamp or rascal.

15. The members of the Dawson Patrol were Inspector F. J. Fitzgerald, Constables G. F. Kinney and J. R. Taylor and Special Constable W. S. Carter. Carter was the ex-Mountie. See R.C. Fetherstonhaugh, *The Royal Canadian Mounted Police* (Garrick & Evans, N.Y., 1938), pp. 160-5.

16. Browning is mistaken. Snow does fall in Sydney but very rarely. See, *The Second Australian Almanac,* (Angus & Robertson, 1986), p. 7.

17. A perusal of available historical records has failed to reveal any information on the second Dawson Patrol. It is possible that the weather was too adverse, but more likely that the idea ran into organisational problems and was abandoned.

18. Browning is quoting from the famous Australian poem by A. B. 'Banjo' Patterson, 'The Man from Snowy River':

And one there was among them on a small and weedy beast
That was something like a racehorse undersized
With a touch of Timor pony, three parts thoroughbred at least
And such as are by mountain horsemen prized

19. The 'White Australia Policy' was the name given to a series of restrictive acts which governed immigration to Australia from Federation until the 1970s. Designed to maintain the Anglo-Saxon and Celtic predominance in Australia, the legislation was designed to deter Asians, Africans and other non-Europeans from applying for entry. Among the more objectionable provisions was a dictation test which could be administered in any language to an applicant. Thus a Chinese whom officials wished to exclude might face a test in Swedish.

20. A quirk of Australian humour is to apply totally inappropriate nicknames – thus, 'Blue' for a redhead, 'Lofty' for a very short person etc.

21. Mayor William Dever.

22. William Morris 'Billy' Hughes was Prime Minister of Australia during World War I. He attempted to introduce conscription for overseas service and it was by attempting to evade this that Browning found himself in the forces. He appears to have retained a lifelong antipathy to Hughes. See references in *'Box Office' Browning.*

23. 'Machine Gun' Jack McGurn (1904-36) was born James Vincenzo De Mora in Chicago's Little Italy and dropped his Italian name in favour of an Irish one when he began his career as a boxer. His father was killed by mobsters over a conflict about supplying sugar to bootleggers. This brought McGurn into action in revenge and he eventually became an 'enforcer' for Al Capone. McGurn was identified as one of the perpetrators of the St Valentine's Day massacre in which seven members of the gang of Capone's rival, George 'Bugs' Moran, were killed, but he was never indicted. Eight years later, on the eve of St Valentine's Day, he was shot to death (with machine guns) in a Chicago bowling alley by two survivors of Moran's old gang.

24. Browning, as was his habit, is reducing his age. Born in 1895, he was around thirty when the events he describes took place.

25. See *'Box Office' Browning* for Elizabeth MacKnight's incriminating information on Browning and also below, p.191.

26. Colonel Roscoe Turner was a fighter pilot in World War I who later established many flying records including a transcontinental crossing record of ten hours, two minutes and fifty-seven seconds. In 1935, flying a high-powered Northrop Gamma, Howard Hughes beat Turner's record by thirty-six minutes. Paul Mantz, one of the first pilots to work regularly in the movies, was technical adviser to aviatrix Amelia Earhart.

27. See Appendix.

28. Marie Dressler was a vaudeville and Broadway actress who made her film debut in Chaplin's *Tilly's Punctured Romance* in 1914. She turned more seriously to films in the 1930s with great success, winning an academy award in 1930. Charles Farrell entered films as an extra in 1923. In the late

twenties and early thirties he made a number of successful romantic films, with Janet Gaynor as his co-star.

29. Another reference to the Melbourne Cup. Spearfelt won the race in 1926.

30. J. T. 'Jack' Lang was a radical Labor politician twice elected Premier of New South Wales, 1925-7 and 1930-2. He passed many social reforms of the kind deplored by MacKnight and attempted to deal with the Depression by adopting Keynesian economic policies greatly feared by conservatives. In 1927 the ACTU (Australian Council of Trade Unions) was formed. The ACTU was intended to act as a Federal governing body over the whole trade union movement. This objective was not achieved but many powerful unions joined the Council.

31. Browning refers to the famous 'long count' incident in the second fight between Dempsey and Tunney. In the seventh round Dempsey knocked Tunney to the canvas with a long left hook. Instead of going to the farthest corner as the rules dictated, Dempsey stood in his own corner, almost directly over his opponent. The referee instructed Dempsey to move; Dempsey argued but eventually complied. The referee then began the count at 'one', although Tunney had been down for four or five seconds. Tunney used the extra time to clear his head and for the remainder of the fight, which he won, he outboxed Dempsey. He got up at 'nine' but may have been down for as long as fourteen seconds.

Also by Peter Corris

'Box Office' Browning

Richard Browning is a crack-shot, six-foot, all-Australian ex-private-school horseman. He is determined to con his way into the new world of filmmaking, but his way to Hollywood is thwarted by World War One, a series of unfortunate affairs and a disastrous marriage. In his developing career as box office poison, Browning makes far more enemies than movies.

'Box Office' Browning is Browning's recollection of his early days from an ungraceful old age. The truth may be filtered through booze, drugs and a lot of years, but the escapades with the famous and the infamous are a delight.

'Beverly Hills' Browning

Richard Browning has a marvellous talent for mucking up even lucky breaks. In fact, he's only really good at one thing; that is, getting away.

Sure, the would-be Aussie movie star makes it to the U.S. of A., but San Francisco proves to be a long way from the starlets, palm trees and swimming pools of Hollywood, at least by the route only he could choose, through Mexico. And then, when he gets to Beverly Hills, he finds bootleggers in the swimming pools, anarchists on the movie sets and starlets just too hot to handle. Not to mention making an enemy of the 'king' of Hollywood, Douglas Fairbanks – the 'city of dreams' becomes nightmare land.

Pokerface

In this thriller the player with the best pokerface wins the game – and it's a dangerous game. Sacked from the shadowy Federal Security Agency, his marriage tottering, Ray Crawley forms an association with radical punk Roxy and her friends – and that's his first mistake.

Crawley's former boss Toby Campion is trying to manipulate him in a game with Canberra. But Crawley is still in the game, and he won't give up. All the players are holding good cards but will the best hand win?

The Baltic Business

'There was a bomb scare,' Crawley said. 'Probably a hoax but whose hoax? They're a weird lot, I can tell you.'

A routine assignment draws Crawley into a web of murder and intrigue involving Eastern European refugees marked by the dark days of the DP camps. His marriage assumes a new dimension as Mandy takes to university study and he takes to the lovely Irina Gilbus whose father heads a shadowy organization known as Nations in Chains.

Set in Melbourne, Peter Corris' thriller features hard-boiled secret-serviceman Ray Crawley and his old mate Huck, the stars of *Pokerface*.

The Kimberley Killing

A routine blood test after a car accident involving a retired Attorney General starts Ray 'Creepy' Crawley and offsider Huck on their latest investigation.

They rleed to delve into the gay sub-culture, though Crawley finds the young widow, Christine Kimberley, far more interesting. The trail moves from Melbourne to Sydney to the Barossa Valley as Crawley and Huck realise they are dealing with some very powerful forces beyond Australia.

The Cargo Club

After a quiet time in Canberra, Crawley is sent to Vitatavu to discredit a government Minister. He becomes involved in the political struggle for control of the island when he is taken hostage by the MMU guerillas. His old mate Huck comes to the rescue but will he be in time . . .

This latest adventure in the *Pokerface* series will be published in 1990.